"It's Like We're Married, Cooper. Only Without Any Of The Good Stuff. Like *Sex*."

He had to admit that up until the night before, he'd never really thought about Kara and sex in the same sentence. But now, he wasn't so sure.

"You want us to have sex?"

"Of course I want sex. But I want more than that, too." Sighing, she said, "I want a husband, kids. A home. I just got so comfortable that I didn't notice that I wasn't getting anywhere."

"What's so bad about comfortable?" he demanded.

"Nothing," she said. "If that's all you're looking for, then comfortable is great. But it's not enough for me. Not anymore."

He knew that once she'd made up her mind about something, that was it.

And the thought of losing Kara hit him hard.

Dear Reader,

Thanks for choosing Silhouette Desire this month. We have a delectable selection of reads for you to enjoy, beginning with our newest installment of THE ELLIOTTS. *Mr. and Mistress* by Heidi Betts is the story of millionaire Cullen Elliott and his mistress who is desperately trying to hide her unexpected pregnancy. Also out this month is the second book of Maureen Child's SUMMER OF SECRETS. *Strictly Lonergan's Business* is a boss/assistant book that will delight you all the way through to its wonderful conclusion.

We are launching a brand-new continuity series this month with SECRET LIVES OF SOCIETY WIVES. The debut title, *The Rags-To-Riches Wife* by Metsy Hingle, tells the story of a working-class woman who has a night of passion with a millionaire and then gets blackmailed into becoming his wife.

We have much more in store for you this month, including Merline Lovelace's *Devlin and the Deep Blue Sea,* part of her cross-line series, CODE NAME: DANGER, in which a feisty female pilot becomes embroiled in a passionate, dangerous relationship. Brenda Jackson is back with a new unforgettable Westmoreland male, in *The Durango Affair.* And Kristi Gold launches a three-book thematic promotion about RICH AND RECLUSIVE men, with *House of Midnight Fantasies.*

Please enjoy all the wonderful books we have for you this month in Silhouette Desire.

Happy reading,

Melissa Jeglinski

Melissa Jeglinski
Senior Editor
Silhouette Books

Please address questions and book requests to:
Silhouette Reader Service
U.S.: 3010 Walden Ave., P.O. Box 1325, Buffalo, NY 14269
Canadian: P.O. Box 609, Fort Erie, Ont. L2A 5X3

MAUREEN CHILD

Strictly Lonergan's Business

Published by Silhouette Books
America's Publisher of Contemporary Romance

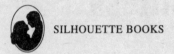 SILHOUETTE BOOKS

ISBN 0-373-76724-2

STRICTLY LONERGAN'S BUSINESS

Copyright © 2006 by Maureen Child

Books by Maureen Child

MAUREEN CHILD

is a California native who loves to travel. Every chance they get, she and her husband are taking off on another research trip. The author of more than sixty books, Maureen loves a happy ending and still swears that she has the best job in the world. She lives in Southern California with her husband, two children and a golden retriever with delusions of grandeur.

To my "other" mother—Mary Ann Child

For everything you've given me.
For everything you've been to me.

I couldn't love you more.

One

"It's really easy," Kara Sloan told herself, giving her own reflection a narrow eyed glare in the rear view mirror. "He opens the door, you say 'I quit.'"

Right.

If it was that easy, she'd have said those two little words six months ago. Heck. A *year* ago.

The minute she'd realized she'd made the huge mistake of falling in love with her employer.

The trouble was, every time she was anywhere near her boss, Cooper Lonergan, her brain shut down and her emotions took over. One look from the man's dark brown eyes and she turned into a puddle of goo.

She still wasn't sure how this had happened.

Heaven knew she hadn't planned it. She'd been the man's assistant for five years, and for four of those five, everything had been great. They'd had a comfortable friendship and easy working relationship. Until it suddenly dawned on her nearly a year ago, that she was in *love* with him.

And ever since that day, she'd been miserable.

She couldn't even get mad at Cooper for not noticing that her feelings had changed. Why would he? To him, she was as familiar a sight in his life as the dark red leather sofa in his living room at home. And just as comfortable.

This situation was her own fault. She'd changed the rules and he didn't even know it. She was in love and he was in like.

Not a good thing.

"Which is *why*," she said sternly, still meeting her own wide green eyes in the rental car mirror, "you have to quit. Just suck it up, face him down and say it."

She inhaled sharply, blew out a breath and nodded grimly. She could do this. She *would* do this.

Muttering darkly, she swung her legs out of the car, slammed the door and then stared up at the big yellow Victorian farmhouse Cooper had rented for the summer. It looked…welcoming, somehow. As if the house had been waiting for her.

Silly, but she was sorry she wouldn't be staying. Sorry she'd have to leave and go back to New York in just two weeks. There was something about this place that 'spoke' to her.

It sat far back on a wide, manicured green lawn and several old shade trees surrounded the structure. Window panes glinted in the morning sunlight, fresh flowers in terra cotta pots lined the porch, their bright summer colors dazzling in the morning light.

She inhaled sharply, deeply, enjoying the scents of freshly mowed grass and the hint of the ocean, just a few miles away. Kara had always considered herself a city girl. Happy in Manhattan, she loved the rush and crush of the crowds, the blaring symphony of horns and shouted insults from the cabbies who drove as if every mile made was a personal victory.

But, she thought, there was something to be said for this, too. The quiet. The color. The lazier pace.

No point in getting used to it, though.

Her three inch heels wobbled slightly on the crushed gravel driveway, and she thought that was only appropriate. Hadn't she been off balance around Cooper all year? Besides, if she'd had any sense, she'd have traveled in jeans and sneakers. But no…she'd had to look *good* when she saw him. Not that he ever noticed what she was wearing.

Gritting her teeth, Kara silently admitted that Cooper wouldn't notice if she had shown up naked.

Which, she reminded herself sternly, was *exactly* why she had to quit her job. It was just too hard. Too miserable to be in love with a man who only saw you as the world's most efficient assistant.

"My own fault," she muttered, turning her back on the house to walk to the rear of the car. She pushed a button on the rental car key ring and the trunk slowly opened like a coffin lid in an old Dracula movie.

They worked well together, had a lot of laughs, and Kara had had the satisfaction of knowing that she did her job so well, he couldn't get along without her. Then she'd messed it all up by changing the rules.

She wasn't even sure when it had happened. When she'd stopped looking at Cooper like an employer and started having X-rated dreams about him. He'd slipped up on her. Sneaked under her defenses. Damn it, he'd made her fall in love with him without even trying and didn't even have the decency to *notice*.

That's why she had to quit. Had to get out while she still could. It was, as her best friend Gina had put it just the night before, *a freaking emergency*.

Gina had taken her out for drinks and given Kara the pep talk that apparently was considered the best friend's duty.

"You know darn well that man is never going to change."

"Why should he?" Kara challenged, stabbing the olive in her martini as if it were an alien out to take over the world. "As far as he's concerned everything is great. Fabulous."

"Exactly my point." Gina blinked at her, lifted one hand to signal the bartender for another round, then turned back to look at her friend again. "He's been in California what? Three days?"

"Yesss…"

"And he's called you like a hundred times already."

True. Her cell phone, always on so that Cooper could get in touch with her whenever he needed to, had been ringing with alarming regularity. Kara checked her watch. Twenty minutes since his last call. He was due. "I work for him."

"Oh, it's way beyond that, Kara," Gina said, leaning across the glossy bar table until her long blond hair brushed the polished surface. "Last time he called, the man asked you how to make *coffee*. He's thirty something and can't make a cup of coffee without your help?"

Kara laughed. "He's thirty one and he can too make coffee. It's just terrible."

Gina was not amused. Shaking her head, she sat back. "You did this to yourself, girlfriend. You made yourself indispensable."

"That's a *bad* thing?" Kara reached for her fresh drink and turned her attention to the new olive.

"It is when Cooper Lonergan sees you like a well-programmed robot." Gina took a gulp of her apple-tini and then waved the glass in the air. "He doesn't see *you*. He never will."

"That's harsh."

"But true."

"Probably."

"So," Gina demanded, "What are you going to do about it? Stick around until you're old and alone and wondering what the hell happened to your life? Or get out now while you still can?"

And *that*, Kara thought now, reaching into the trunk, is the million dollar question. She knew Gina was right. Heck, she'd known the truth for the last year. She had no future with Cooper. At least, nothing beyond what she had now. And that just wasn't enough.

Not anymore.

A crisp, cool wind with the scent of the sea on it, swept across the yard, set the leaves on the trees dancing, and tossed her dark brown hair across her eyes. She plucked it back, blew out a breath and grabbed up both her suitcase, the small carry-on bag she'd filled with fresh bagels from Cooper's favorite deli, the gourmet coffee he couldn't write without, and five bags of marshmallow cookies.

The man had the palate of a ten-year-old. She smiled to herself, thinking, as she always did, that it was kind of cute how Cooper had to have his favorite cookies on hand at all times.

But she caught herself an instant later. Not cute. Annoying. Right.

Nodding to herself, she pledged that the minute she saw Cooper, she'd give him notice. Two weeks.

He could hire someone temporarily for this summer in California, then when he went home to Manhattan, he could find a more permanent replacement.

As for Kara, the sooner she got back to New York and what was left of her life…the better.

Grim determination fed her steps as she started toward the big house at the end of drive. With every wobble of her heels, she told herself over and over, *It's just a job. You can find another, better one. You don't need Cooper.*

She'd almost convinced herself when the front door flew open, the ancient screen door slapped against the wall of the house and Cooper Lonergan stepped out onto the wide front porch.

Tall and lean, he was wearing his New York uniform of black pants and black shirt. His features were sharp, angular and his black hair, just long enough to touch his shoulders, flew about his face like a dirty halo. His dark eyes glinted in the sun and when he smiled, Kara felt it deliver a solid punch to her belly. Probably had more impact because he didn't really smile all that often. But brother, when he did…

The man was mouthwatering.

Damn it.

"Kara!" He took the five steps down to the yard in two long strides and crossed to where she was still standing, dumbstruck by the force of her own emotions. He swept her up into a brief, hard hug that lit up her insides like Times Square on New Year's Eve, then let her go so abruptly, she staggered back a step.

"Thank God you're here."

A brief flash of something that might have been hope darted through her. "You missed me?"

"Boy, did I," he said. "You have no idea. I made coffee this morning and it pretty much tasted like I think motor oil with a dash of cinnamon would taste."

Right. Hope dissolved into reality. Of course he hadn't actually missed her. When she took her three weeks of vacation every year, he didn't miss *her*. He missed the convenience of having her around. Why should this time be any different?

"Please tell me you brought real coffee and my cookies."

She sighed, accepting the truth. "Yes Cooper, you too tall four-year-old. I have the coffee and I brought your cookies."

"Excellent." He ignored her jibe, just as he pretty much ignored her, Kara thought. Then he took her suitcase from her and started for the house. "Did you get the dry cleaning for me, too?"

"It's in the trunk."

"And bagels. Oh God, tell me you remembered the bagels."

She shook her head and kept pace with him. Ten seconds with him and she fell into the old, familiar pattern. What had happened to her vow? Where had her backbone gone? Why wasn't she looking into those dark chocolate eyes of his and telling him that she quit?

She took a breath and almost groaned. He even *smelled* delicious.

"Yes, I remembered the bagels," she muttered, disgusted with both of them. "When in the last five years have I *not* remembered?"

"Never," he said with a quick wink that weakened her knees even as it stiffened what was left of her resolve. "That's why I can't live without you."

Words spoken so easily, so lightly. She knew it meant nothing to him, but if they were only true, what those words would mean to her.

Cooper ushered Kara into the house, standing back to let her pass in front of him. Her heels clicked against the wood floor and she flipped her long, dark brown hair back over her shoulder as she turned in a circle to look around the room.

He took his first good look at the same time. Sure, he'd been there three days already, but he'd spent most of his time in the master bedroom, sitting at a makeshift desk, working.

Well, *trying* to work. In reality, he'd played about three thousand games of solitaire. Which wouldn't help him meet the deadline that was already flying at him.

"It's a great place," Kara said, studying an old brass chandelier hanging in the center of the living room.

He glanced around, noting the big, overstuffed

chairs in faded cabbage rose upholstery. A braided rug covered most of the scarred wood floor and the pale yellow walls looked bright and cheerful, even to him. The property management company who'd leased the place to him had done a first-rate job keeping the old house in shape.

"People say it's haunted."

She whipped around and stared at him, her green eyes wide and fascinated. "It is?"

He nodded. "When I was a kid, I spent every summer here in Coleville with my grandfather and my cousins." Memories rushed in, nearly strangling him with the force of the accompanying emotions. He pushed them down, deliberately shut the door on the feelings rising in him as he said, "We'd ride our bikes over here at night and watch this house, tell each other scary stories and wait to see something otherworldly floating by." He shrugged and smiled. "We never saw a damn thing."

"And since you've been here…?"

"Nada."

"Well that's disappointing," Kara said.

He smiled at the whine in her voice. No matter what, he could always count on Kara to see the same possibilities that he could. As a horror novelist, he'd really enjoyed the idea of renting the same haunted house that had fascinated him as a kid.

But he should have known that the only ghosts he'd find this summer were those in his own past. Instinctively, Cooper cut that thought off neatly. He wasn't going to go there.

"Anyway," Cooper said with a shrug, "It's only a couple of miles from my grandfather's place, so it was handy."

"Oh! How is your grandfather?"

"Long story. But he's actually fine."

"But his doctor said he was dying…"

"Like I said," Cooper repeated, not really wanting to go into it all at the moment. "Long story. First, tell me what took you so long to get here. I expected you yesterday."

"I told you it would take three days to close up your condo and take care of all the details—"

"You're right, you did. Just felt like a really *long* three days. You're the best, Kara. Have I given you a raise lately?"

"No," she chided.

"Put that on your list—" he cut her off before she could say anything else. "The important thing is you're here now."

She smiled at him and Cooper added, "With you here, I can finally work. I'm telling you, I haven't had a decent meal since I left home."

Her smile slowly faded.

"The grocery store in Coleville doesn't deliver, so you'll need to make a trip over there to stock up." He picked up her suitcase and headed for the stairs. "I'll put your bags away. You're in the room across from mine. It's big, got a nice view of the fields. We have to share the bathroom, but we'll work it out. You could make up a schedule and—"

"Cooper!"

He paused, looked back at her and sent her another one of those rare, genuine smiles. "It really is good to see you, Kara. And it's okay. I know what you're gonna say."

"Really?"

"Absolutely," he said. "I feel the same way. Good to have things back to normal."

Two

A few hours later, Kara had been to the grocery store, had a chicken roasting in the oven and had even managed to arrange for a fax machine to be delivered and set up first thing tomorrow.

Cooper was upstairs working and down here, in the square, farmhouse style kitchen, Kara was wondering what the heck had happened to her plan.

She hitched one hip against the worn, Formica countertop and folded both arms across her chest. Wearing her favorite pair of faded, nearly threadbare jeans, a pale blue T-shirt and wonderful, comfortable sneakers, she shook her head and said aloud, "You're a wimp, Kara. A spineless wiener dog. A disgrace to assistants everywhere."

Late afternoon sunlight slanted through the curtained window, making lacy shadows on the round, pedestal table and the gleaming wood floor. Kara watched as a soft breeze ruffled the curtains, sending those shadows into a lazy dance.

Walking across the room, she pulled out one of the captain's chairs and plopped down onto it. Bracing her elbows on the table, she stared out through a gap in the curtains at the rolling back lawn that stretched out to a wide green field. Then she heaved a dramatic sigh of complete disgust. Oh, she wasn't disgusted with Cooper so much as she was with herself.

Back to normal. Abruptly, she shifted in the chair, leaned back and stretched out her fingertips. Her nails tapped against the table like a frantic heartbeat. "Not his fault he fell right back into the same pattern we've been in for years. You *knew* this was going to happen, Kara. The question is…why didn't you quit?"

But she knew the answer to that already. Because one look at Cooper and her fantasies took over. Her reasonable, intelligent, logical brain went right to sleep and into Fantasy Land.

She'd imagined it all so perfectly, her dreams were even filled with the dialogue her brain had provided. And sitting right there at the kitchen table, she indulged herself yet one more time. She'd walk into a room, a stray beam of sunlight would strike her just so and...

Cooper glances up. His gaze meets hers. And for one, heart-stopping moment, the two of them are lost in the suddenly discovered rush of love.

He crosses the room to her, cups her face in his big, wonderful hands and says, "My God, Kara. How could I have been so stupid? How could I not have seen the real you for so long? Can you ever forgive me?"

And Kara smiles, reaches up to cover his hands with her own and says, "There's nothing to forgive. It's enough that we're finally together. I love you, Cooper."

He whispers "I love you, too," just before he kisses her with more passion than she could have imagined.

"Right," she muttered now, coming up out of her daydream like a drowning diver frantically breaching the water's surface to find air. "*Nothing to forgive?* What am I? An idiot?"

Yes, she thought. An idiot in love with a man who was clueless enough to not even notice what was right in front of him. A man who would *never* see her until it was too late.

A sigh swept through the room.

Kara jolted upright and twisted her head from side to side, glancing around the empty kitchen, futilely trying to find the source of that heartbreaking sound. But there was nothing. She stiffened, waiting for it to come again. It didn't. There was just a sunny kitchen, empty but for her. Chills snaked along Kara's spine and tingled at the base of her neck.

A ghost?

Cooper did tell her the house was supposedly haunted. But then he'd also said he hadn't felt a thing in three days.

"Imagination," she whispered, standing up slowly, carefully. She chuckled softly, and pretended that her laughter didn't sound quite as shaky as it felt. Swallowing hard, she rubbed her hands up and down her arms, dispelling the sensation of every nerve in her body standing on end.

Then, blaming the weird feeling on her own day-dreaming, Kara shut down her brain and finished getting dinner ready.

Cooper spent his day with a murderous demon.

His mind raced just a few beats ahead of his fingers, furiously typing at the keyboard. He knew what he wanted to capture. What he wanted his reader to feel. What surprised him was that this was the first piece of decent writing he'd managed to accomplish since arriving in California. It felt good. Good to be lost in his own imagination. Good to be caught up by the characters forming on his computer screen.

Good to let go—however briefly—of the memories that had been choking him for three long days.

A silent shroud of snow covered the walkway to the old hotel, but David hardly noticed. The cold seeped into his bones, down to his soul and a ribbon of dread slowly unwound in the pit of his stomach. His shoulders hunched against the icy wind, he shuffled his steps, reluctant to approach, as if every cell in his body was trying to warn him to stay away...

Cooper finally lifted his fingers from the computer keyboard and leaned back in his desk chair. He knew exactly how the hero of his latest novel felt. Hadn't he himself only reluctantly returned to Coleville? Wasn't every cell in *his* body still telling him to get the hell out?

But he was trapped for the summer. No getting out of it. He'd given his word to his grandfather, and a Lonergan never went back on his word. Even to sneaky old men who lie to their grandsons about being at death's door on a skateboard.

Not that he was pissed off about that, he assured himself. He was glad Jeremiah wasn't dying. Glad the old man was as healthy and apparently, as slippery as he'd always been. But damn it, Cooper hadn't been back to Coleville in fifteen years. And if Jeremiah hadn't pulled one over on him, he doubted he ever would have returned.

It was too hard. Too many memories, constantly

fluttering through his mind like swarms of gnats—annoying and impossible to ignore.

His screen saver flicked on, a haunted house complete with bats, ghosts and vampires. Usually, that was enough to motivate him to get back to writing. To delve into whatever story he had going. Today though, he ignored the animated cartoon drawing filling the screen.

From downstairs came the clank of pans and the rush of water through old pipes. The scent of something delicious wafted up the stairs and he took a deep breath, enjoying not only the mingled aromas of garlic and sage, but the realization that Kara was right downstairs.

Damn, it was good having Kara here. And for more reasons than her cooking abilities.

Since arriving in Coleville for the first time in fifteen years, Cooper had never felt so alone. Sure, his family was right down the road a couple of miles, but here, in this house, he lay alone at night and felt emptiness crowding in on him.

Ordinarily, he liked being alone. In New York, he spent most days working, avoiding the phone, the doorbell, and e-mail. Kara kept the world at bay, affording him plenty of time to lose himself in his stories. When he needed a distraction, the city was just beyond his doorstep and there were any number of women he could call.

Here though, the quiet reigned supreme. There

were no hustling throngs of people. No loud crash and scream of cabs darting in and out of vicious traffic. No sirens or street peddlers. Just the quiet— and too much time to think.

Pushing his chair back, Cooper stood up and walked across his bedroom to the window overlooking the front of the house. He wasn't seeing the neatly tended yard, or the shade trees, or even the green field sweeping down the narrow two lane road toward his grandfather's ranch.

As he had the last three days, he looked beyond, to a lake he couldn't even see from here. He'd thought that renting a house a couple of miles away would be enough. That not being able to actually *see* the water would make being here easier.

But he should have known better.

Hell, he'd been living in Manhattan for years, and every night in his dreams, he saw that lake. Every day when he sat down to write the horror novels that had given him fame and fortune, he saw that lake. Saw again how that summer day fifteen years ago had become a nightmare.

If he closed his eyes now, it would all come racing back. The feel of the sun on bare shoulders. The rush of laughter from his cousins. The sigh of wind in the trees. The splash as he and his cousins had taken turns jumping for distance into the icy water.

The numbing shock that followed.

So he didn't close his eyes, but the memories clung to the edges of his mind, taunting him, pushing at him. He reached up, scraped one hand through his hair, then rubbed his eyes as if he could rub away the images that felt as though they were burned on his retinas.

"Hey!"

Startled, he spun around and found Kara standing in the open doorway staring at him. Heart pounding, he shook his head and scowled at her. "Trying to give me a heart attack?"

"It wasn't on the schedule for tonight, no," she said and stepped into the room, still watching him curiously. "Everything okay?"

No.

"Why wouldn't it be?" he hedged and turned his back on her to walk back to the desk and his laptop. He never left the lid up when someone else was around. Call it superstition or whatever, he didn't like anyone getting a peek at what he was working on.

"Well, because I called your name three times and you didn't hear me."

"I was…thinking," he said and at least it wasn't a lie.

"New book giving you trouble?"

"Yeah." His fingertips smoothed over the gray lid of the computer as if caressing the words hidden inside. "At least, it was. Until today." He forced a smile as he looked at her. "You must have brought me some luck."

"Uh-huh." She crossed the room, threw the curtains back and opened the window. A cold sharp breeze raced into the room as if it had been crouched just outside, waiting its chance. "So, translation is, you didn't work before because I wasn't here."

"Right." Cooper watched her as she wandered the room, efficiently tidying up the space, folding the old quilt at the foot of his bed, straightening a framed landscape, then turning to the desk, where she shuffled papers into neat stacks.

He felt calmer just watching her. Damn, Kara was good for him. She always had been. Her voice, her even temper, her cool logic, her no-nonsense way of looking at the world was exactly the right leash he needed to keep him grounded.

"So I'm guessing," she said, glancing at him with a knowing gleam in her eye, "that means you killed me horribly again."

One corner of his mouth quirked into a half smile. God, she knew him better than anyone ever had. Part of the fun of being a writer was being able to kill off whomever happened to be bugging you at the time. And when Kara wasn't around, it was lowering to admit just how lost he felt without her. Hence the catharsis of killing off a secretary/assistant in one of his stories.

"How'd I die this time?" she asked, planting both hands on her hips. "Drowning?"

"I told you before," he said, his voice going as stiff as his spine. "*You* never drown."

"Okay," she said, lifting both hands in mock surrender. "Sheesh. Just asked."

"Right. Sorry." He pushed one hand through his hair again and willed the tremor inside into stillness.

In every one of his books, at least one character drowned. But it was always someone Cooper didn't like. Someone he thought the readers wouldn't be too invested in. Death by drowning was something Cooper could never take lightly. Not with his memories. Not with the past that was always so close.

"You sure you're okay?"

"Yeah," he said, nodding as if to confirm his own word. "I'm fine. Did you come up here for something in particular?"

"Dinner's ready."

He glanced at the window. The sun was just setting. Turning his gaze back to her he asked, "This early?"

"Shoot me, I'm hungry." Shrugging, Kara headed for the door and said over her shoulder, "You can wait till later if you want to."

"No," he said, sweeping his gaze around the room that without her suddenly seemed way too empty. "I'll join you."

"Great. You can open the bottle of chardonnay I got at the market."

He chuckled as he followed her downstairs.

"Mmm. Chardonnay from Al's market in Coleville, California. Can't wait."

"Snob."

"Peasant."

Kara was still laughing as they walked into the kitchen. She took a seat at the table and watched him as he grabbed the wine and the bottle opener. They'd already settled back into the familiar routine. And damn it, it felt good. And right.

God, she would miss this so much when she left. And she *had* to leave. That was more apparent by the moment. They'd become too comfortable together.

He sat down and his long legs bumped into hers. Kara felt a flash of something hot and dazzling skyrocket inside, and only just managed to keep from yelping.

Naturally, Cooper didn't notice.

While he poured clear, straw colored wine into the pink antique glasses she'd found in a cupboard, Kara looked around at the homey old kitchen. The cabinets were painted white, the appliances looked as though they were new in the fifties, and the windows overlooked a huge backyard lined by ancient shade trees.

It all should have been…soothing somehow. Cozy. Instead though, Kara felt a sensation of…waiting. She hadn't heard anything weird since that sigh earlier in the afternoon and she'd almost convinced herself that hadn't really happened.

"This smells great," Cooper said, helping himself to a serving of chicken, potatoes and fresh broccoli.

"You know you could have found the grocery store yourself," Kara pointed out, taking a sip of her wine. Cool, tart, wonderful.

"Oh, I did," he said, reaching for a slice of wheat bread from the plate in the center of the table. "I bought coffee and a couple boxes of doughnuts. Oh," he added, "and a few frozen burritos."

"Pitiful." And somehow, cute. How twisted was she?

"We go with our strengths," he said around a bite of chicken. Then his dark eyes closed and he sighed, obviously in pure heaven. "At home, I can call a restaurant. Here—let's just say that the Burger Hut doesn't deliver." He swallowed and groaned. "Man, Kara. I owe you. Big."

She didn't want him to owe her.

She wanted him to *love* her.

But she might as well wish for a ten pound weight loss and a spanking new wardrobe by morning. Neither wish was going to happen.

Outside, late afternoon slid into twilight, the sky softly darkening. Inside, a familiar, comfortable silence settled between them and Kara found herself taking mental pictures that she would be able to pull out and look at later—after she left.

At that thought, her gaze landed on Cooper and a twinge of regret pinged off her chest, bouncing off her heart, leaving it feeling bruised. She hated the notion of walking out of Cooper's life, but at the same time, she had to, if she ever expected to get a life of her own.

Still, she wanted to enjoy what time she did have with him, so she pushed those thoughts to the back of her mind and asked, "So, what's the story on your grandfather?"

He grabbed his wineglass and took a long drink. Then he eyed the liquid in surprise. "Pretty good."

"Uh-huh," she said, sensing a stall tactic. "Talk."

"Right." While he ate, he told her the story of Jeremiah's tricky maneuvers to get his grandsons back home for the summer. Not only had Jeremiah faked a bad heart, he'd even convinced his own doctor to go along with the deception. He'd worried them all, just to get them to come back to Coleville.

"That's terrible," Kara said.

"Yeah," Cooper agreed, taking another bite of chicken. "Jeremiah's a wily old goat. But this was pretty low. He scared the hell out of us."

"No," Kara said, glaring at him because he couldn't see what she was trying to say. "I *meant* it was terrible that your grandfather felt as though he had no choice but to coerce his grandsons into a visit."

"Huh?" His dark eyes fixed on her in confusion.

"How could you all do that to him, Cooper?" She set her fork down on her plate and the quiet *clink* it made sounded overly loud in the suddenly still room.

The silence only lasted for a moment or two.

"*We* didn't do anything," he pointed out defensively, waving his own fork at her for emphasis.

"That's the point," she said, taking a gulp of wine and letting the icy liquid slide down her throat to form a nice warm ball in the pit of her stomach. "You didn't do anything. None of you."

"Hey."

"You said you haven't been back here in fifteen years, Cooper."

"There were reasons."

"*Reasons?* For breaking an old man's heart?" Sympathy welled inside her and along with it came anger. "You went away and stayed away. The poor man. No wonder he was desperate enough to lie."

He sighed and sat back in his chair, gripping his wineglass as if it were a life rope. "You're right."

"What?" She thunked the heel of her hand above her right ear. "I mean, excuse me?"

"Funny," he acknowledged with a nod. "But you heard me. I know we were wrong to stay away so long. Trust me, it wasn't easy on any of us, either. Don't you think we missed Jeremiah? Don't you think it was hard for us to stay away?"

"Then why?" she whispered, leaning on the table to watch him carefully. "Why did it take you so long to come home for a visit?"

"Because, Kara," he said softly, shifting his gaze from hers to the surface of the pale wine in his glass.

"As hard as it was to stay away, it was even harder to come back here."

There was something distant about Cooper. As if he had emotionally taken one giant step back from her. As if he were deliberately trying to shut her out. And it hurt. They'd been close for five years. She'd thought they were, if not lovers, then at least friends.

"Cooper…" she waited for him to look at her. As stubborn as he could be, she kept quiet, counting the ticking seconds as they passed before, at last, his gaze lifted to hers. Those dark brown eyes looked shadowed by old pain and instantly she felt an answering ache inside her. "What could be so important that it would keep you from someone you love for so long?"

He took a sip of wine, swallowed, then set the glass carefully onto the table as if afraid it would shatter.

"Sometimes love's just not enough, Kara." He sighed, scraped one hand across his face, then forced a smile that did nothing to ease the shadows in his eyes. "Sometimes love is the problem."

An icy draft slipped through the kitchen, twining itself around Kara, reaching out for Cooper and then holding them both in a chill embrace.

"Whoa," Cooper said as Kara shivered, "these old places really let in the cold." He stood up and started across the kitchen. "I'll close the living room windows."

The cold eased away and Kara sent a disquieted glance around the empty room. Old houses were drafty, yes. But Cooper's errand was a fruitless one. She'd closed the windows herself an hour ago.

Three

Kara woke up with a jolt.

Heart pounding, lungs heaving, she shook off the last of the nightmare still clinging to the edges of her mind. She swallowed hard and grabbed at the quilt pooled at her waist in an effort to steady herself.

She couldn't remember what she'd been dreaming. Couldn't remember what had chased her from that dream into wakefulness. All she *did* know was that goose bumps were racing up and down her spine and air was still hard to come by.

Then she heard it.

Sobbing.

Someone in the old house was crying as if their

heart was breaking. The sound lifted, rising, filling the house with pain that was nearly tangible. Then an instant later, the sobs quieted, becoming a whisper that Kara strained to hear.

Mouth dry, heartbeat frantic, she tossed the quilt back and swung her legs to the floor. The polished wooden floorboards felt cold against her bare feet, but she hardly noticed. She moved to the door, determined to follow the desperate sobs to their source.

Fear tugged at her insides, but curiosity was stronger. Grabbing hold of the icy brass knob, she opened her door, stepped into the hallway and stopped dead. The sorrow filled wails rose again, and with them, the small hairs at the back of Kara's neck.

Moonlight filtered in through the arch-shaped window at the end of the hall, painting a pale silver glow on the walls and the faded carpet runner stretched down the center of the hallway. Outside, trees danced in the wind and their shadows dipped and swayed wildly.

Kara could have sworn she jumped three feet, straight up, when the door across from hers suddenly swung open. Heart in her throat now, she grabbed hold of the doorjamb as Cooper appeared on the threshold. His long black hair mussed from sleep, he glared at the empty hallway, then at her.

"What the hell is going on around here?" he demanded, voice raw.

She had to swallow hard before she could be sure

her voice would work. He wore dark red cotton drawstring pants that hung low on his hips and the hems stacked up on his bare feet. In the moonlight, his sculpted chest looked as if it had been lovingly molded from a sheet of bronze and Kara's palms itched to touch it. Touch him.

"Kara?" He waved one hand in front of her face to get her attention. "Hello?"

She shook her head, told her hormones to take a vacation and snapped, "Get your hand out of my face, Cooper."

"You zoned out on me."

"I did not *zone out*," she argued, though she was pretty sure she had. Heck, one long look at Cooper, fresh from bed, was enough to conquer the strongest of women. And Kara had already admitted to being a spineless wiener dog.

The sobbing rose again, swelling up from below the stairs like a slowly inflating balloon taking to the sky. And a new set of goose pimples ice-skated up and down Kara's arms.

Cooper turned his head and stared at the head of the stairs for a long minute, before turning his gaze back to her. "Tell me you heard that."

She huffed out an anxious breath. "Oh, yeah."

"Good."

"*Good?*" she repeated. "What's *good* about that?"

"I thought I was dreaming it," he whispered, stepping further into the hall and throwing another glance at the stairs. "Then I figured it was a hallucination. But if we're both hearing it, then that means it's real." His voice dropped even further and he leaned in close so she could hear him above the mournful weeping that seemed to be dripping from the walls. "And if it's real, then somebody's trying to pull something funny."

Kara swallowed hard. Cooper's breath came warm against her cheek and she had to fight to concentrate on what he was saying instead of the way he made her feel, leaning in so darn close. Closing her eyes briefly, she gulped at air then asked, "Who would think this kind of thing is funny?"

He shot her a look. "My cousin Jake for one, but as far as I know he's still in Spain." Then he smiled. "Mike Haney."

"Who?" Kara followed him quietly, walking right behind him as he started down the center of the hall toward the stairs.

He turned around quickly and she nearly yelped.

"Shhh…" he said, dropping both hands onto her shoulders. "Mike Haney's an old friend. We all grew up together. My cousin Sam told me he saw ol' Mike in town the other day. And trust me, this is *just* the kind of thing Mike would think up."

She didn't think so. But then, her brain wasn't really working on all cylinders at the moment. His big hands, with those talented, long fingers, held her firmly and felt so warm on her skin. Everything inside her hummed with an electrical sort of awakening that couldn't be quenched—even by the goose bumps that were still rippling along her spine.

Focus, Kara, focus.

"Cooper—"

"Stay here," he warned, lifting one hand to hold up his index finger like he was signaling a recalcitrant puppy to sit.

"Excuse me?"

He scowled. "Kara, will you just stay here while I go down and beat the crap outta Mike?"

"No, I'm not staying here," she said and waved a hand, silently telling him to get going and she'd be right behind him. "What? Are we in a 1950s movie? Big strong man leaves the little woman behind while he stalks off to danger?"

He snorted. "The only one in danger around here is Mike Haney."

"That sobbing does *not* sound like a guy."

He looked about to argue, so she added, "Besides, what if you're wrong? You think I want to be up here all by myself? No freakin' way."

The crying continued, rolling on and on, lifting and falling like waves cresting on the shore, then sliding back out to sea. The very air seemed thicker, heavier somehow and Kara—for just a second and who could really blame her—almost wanted to be in that old movie. Hiding under a bed while Cooper went to check things out.

Then a terrible, wrenching moan swept through the house and Kara's heart twisted in empathy.

"Stay behind me," Cooper muttered, starting down the stairs at a dead creep, carefully putting one foot gently down before moving the other.

"No problem there," she murmured and stayed as close to him as his shadow at high noon.

He reached behind him, grabbed her hand in his and held on tight. Kara clung to him like he was the last eighty percent off sweater at a clearance sale at Bloomie's.

At the bottom of the stairs, the sound was all around them, reverberating off the walls, the floor, the ceilings, until it seemed to echo over and over again.

"Cooper…"

"Come on…"

His legs were a lot longer than hers, so Kara practically had to trot to keep up with him as he sprinted for the main parlor.

"It's centered there," he whispered. "You hear it? Louder the closer we get."

And now that they were almost on top of the sound, Kara wondered why in the devil she'd wanted to come down here to investigate it in the first place. If it *was* a friend of Cooper's, then there was nothing to worry about. And if it *wasn't?* Oh, she so didn't want to think about that at the moment.

"Ready?" He glanced at her as his left hand curled around the brass knob of the parlor door.

"No."

He shot her a wicked grin that quieted her fear and stirred up other, far more interesting things. She nodded jerkily. "Fine. Just open it."

He did. Throwing the door wide open, Cooper dragged Kara into the room behind him.

Instantly, the sobbing stopped.

Moonlight slanted through the wide front windows, illuminating the tiny room like someone in heaven was focusing a spotlight on the place. Deep shadows crouched in the corners, but when Cooper flicked on the overhead chandelier, they disappeared. Kara and Cooper were alone in the room.

Loosening his grip on her hand, Cooper stalked around the perimeter of the small, old fashioned parlor. He pulled back the drapes at either side of the windows and even opened an old armoire, as if expecting to find Mike Haney and a tape recorder, crouched inside.

When he found nothing, he turned around and looked at Kara. "Okay, I admit it, I'm stumped."

Kara wandered the room more slowly, touching the little china dog on an end table, smoothing her fingertips across the fringe on a lampshade. Thoughtfully, she asked, "You said the place was haunted, right?"

Cooper frowned, folded his arms across his chest and watched her. He'd been so sure that either Sam or Mike was at the bottom of this night's little spookfest. Hadn't they all enjoyed scaring the crap out of each other when they were kids? And what better thing to do to a horror writer then give him his very own personal ghost?

But if his cousin and friend were behind it, where was the proof? Of course, he'd have to give the room a thorough going over in the morning, but at the moment, he couldn't figure out how that voice was pumped through the whole damn house and then cut off in an instant.

"Just because I didn't find Mike hiding in here," Cooper said, "doesn't mean there's a ghost in the house."

"Uh-huh."

She didn't look convinced. As she wandered around the room, studying the spines of the worn leather books tucked into a bookcase, Cooper studied her. He hadn't noticed before—now, he couldn't imagine why not—but, Kara's sleep ruffled dark brown hair hung in unruly waves to her shoulders. The summery, pale green silk nightgown she wore had thin straps and dipped low across her breasts before skimming a surprisingly taut, tempting body and ending just beneath the curve of her behind. Her legs were bare and her toenails were painted a brilliant scarlet.

Heat slammed into him and Cooper whooshed out a breath in reaction. His gaze locked on her as she stooped down to inspect a book on a lower shelf and he caught himself hoping she'd simply bend over.

Man.

Where the hell had that come from?

In the five years he'd known and worked with Kara Sloane, Cooper could honestly say he'd never once been slapped with the notion of tossing her over his shoulder and throwing her onto the nearest bed.

Now, it was the only thought in his fevered mind.

"Are you okay?"

"Hmm?" He shook his head and scowled even more fiercely when he found her watching him curiously. Great. Could she tell he'd been wondering if she was wearing anything underneath that nightgown? "Of course I'm okay. Why wouldn't I be?"

"No reason," she said, in a tone that clearly contradicted her words, "you were just…looking at me weird."

He forced a laugh that grated his throat and sounded overly loud. "No I wasn't."

"Yeah, you were."

Smooth, Cooper. Really smooth. He stabbed both hands through his hair and gave it a tug while he was at it. Anything to distract him from the thoughts that were now racing uncontrollably through his brain. Kara in that nightgown. Kara *out* of that nightgown. Geez.

"Didn't mean to," he said with a careless shrug, "it's just, you look…different."

"*Different?*" She folded her arms beneath her breasts, thereby pushing them high enough to peek over the top of that low scooped neck.

Cooper felt what was left of the blood in his brain rush southward.

"Never mind," he muttered and turned to check all the windows, making sure the latches were closed. *Keep busy. Don't think. Don't…*

"Different how?"

He glanced at her over his shoulder and immediately turned back around. She was suddenly looking *way* too good. And his own body was starting to get *very* appreciative. "Leave it alone, will ya?"

"Nope. *Different how?*" Amusement colored her voice and Cooper winced.

Sighing, he admitted stiffly, "The nightgown."

She chuckled and he turned to look at her, keeping his gaze locked with hers, for his own peace of mind.

"My nightgown? Honestly, Cooper," she said, skimming her hands along the silky fabric barely covering her. "It's not like I'm wearing black lace."

Mmm. A picture burst into life in his mind and he enjoyed it far too much.

"Besides," she added, "I was sleeping. What? Did you really think I wore high heels to bed?"

Yet *another* interesting image filled his brain and left him inwardly groaning. Seriously. Between the weird noises and the new visuals of Kara, he was probably going to be awake all night.

He blew out a long breath and determinedly shifted the subject away from Kara's nightgown. "We're not going to figure out what's happening tonight and I'm too tired—" translation, *horny*, "—to talk about this anymore. Let's just forget about it and go back to sleep."

The smile slid off her face as her gaze swept the quiet, empty room. "You think it'll start up again?"

"I sincerely hope not," he muttered and led the way out of the room. He heard her walking behind him, the soft fall of her small bare feet against the floorboards. At the foot of the stairs, he started taking them two at a time. No way was he going to climb those stairs behind Kara.

The view would kill him.

The next day, as Kara sat beside Cooper in his enormous SUV, she was still enjoying the sensation of having finally won his attention. However briefly it had lasted. She'd seen his face the night before. Watched him watch her and though she knew nothing would come of it, she'd relished the few moments when he'd looked at her and really seen her.

Of course it wouldn't happen again.

Without the quiet intimacy of a shadow filled house in the middle of the night, everything was back to normal. Cooper, kind but distracted, Kara, wishing things were different.

He'd avoided her all morning. When he came down for coffee, he'd simply nodded at her, then filled a thermal jug so he wouldn't have to face her again. She'd heard his fingers flying across the keyboard, but except for that constant sound, whispering in the background, she might as well have been alone in the house. Well, just she and whoever had done all the crying the night before.

And now, though he was sitting less than a foot away from her, he still wasn't talking. Instead, he kept his gaze locked on the road and determinedly away from her.

She simply could not go on like this forever.

She wanted a man to love her. She wanted children before she was old enough to be a grandmother.

Slanting a look at him now as he steered his car into the driveway of his grandfather's ranch, she watched as his features tightened. His dark eyes narrowed and a muscle in his jaw twitched as if he were gritting his teeth.

What was it? Why was he so reluctant to be here? To see an old man she knew he loved?

And why wouldn't he tell her?

The SUV sailed smoothly over the rutted road with hardly a bump to the occupants. Cooper drove around behind the edge of the house and parked the car under the shade of a giant tree that looked as though it had been there since the beginning of time.

Wind scuttled across the open yard, lifting dust and tossing it into tiny tornadoes while it fluttered the laundry dancing on the clothesline. Ancient shade trees lined the property, swaying in that same wind, sliding in from the nearby ocean.

There was a small guesthouse at the edge of the yard and even from a distance, Kara could see the sunlight glinting off shining window panes. Pansies in shades of deep purple and blue tumbled from a window box near the tidy front porch and a grape-vine wreath with a tiny Welcome sign attached hung on the door.

About a hundred yards from the main house, a barn stood proudly, its double doors standing open, inviting visitors into the cool, shadowy interior.

But the house itself caught Kara's attention. It was old and proud and wide. It sprawled across the land like a lazy old man stretched out for a nap. Stone pillars guarded the four corners of the house and bright red and white geraniums crowded the outside edges of the structure. It looked, Kara thought, permanent. Cozy.

Apparently though, it looked like something else entirely to Cooper. Shutting off the engine, he pulled the keys from the car and jangled them in his palm for a second or two.

They'd been invited to his grandfather's house for lunch, but never had a man looked less willing to go inside a relative's home.

Finally, Kara asked, "Are you okay?"

"Fine," he said shortly. "Why?"

"I don't know," she answered, "because there's enough tension rolling off of you right now to make diamonds out of charcoal?"

He sighed and leaned back, unbuckling his seat belt but making no move to get out of the car. Turning his head, he looked at her for the first time that morning. In his eyes, Kara saw a tumult of emotions that appeared and disappeared so quickly, she couldn't identify them all.

And for the first time since she'd known him, she was worried about Cooper. There was something here. Something that was tearing at him.

"It's not something I want to talk about."

Intrigued, and a little unsettled, Kara unsnapped her own seat belt and shifted in her seat to look at him. "But if there's something I should know before I meet your family..."

He smiled briefly, the slightest curve of his lips and then it was gone again. "Don't worry," he said, opening the car door. "They don't want to talk about it, either."

Four

Cooper watched his cousin Sam wink at his new fiancée Maggie and felt a twinge of something suspiciously like envy. Which didn't really make any sense at all, because he'd never wanted the whole "wife and family" thing anyway. And yet...

Lunch had been awkward, despite Jeremiah's repeated attempts to keep everyone talking, laughing. Cooper had been uneasy from the moment he'd stepped into his grandfather's house. For some insane reason, he'd kept waiting for a sixteen-year-old Mac to come running into the room—and when he didn't, the pain roared through Cooper, as hot and fresh as it had been fifteen years before.

Now that he was outside, sitting in a lawn chair at the back of the house, Cooper at least felt as though he could breathe again. But the memories here were just as thick. Still watching Sam, in the chair beside him, he blurted suddenly, "How can you do it?"

"Do what?" Sam reluctantly tore his gaze from Maggie, hanging damp sheets on the clothesline.

"Be here," Cooper said, clutching his beer bottle in one tight fist and sweeping his arm out to encompass the ranch. "*Live* here."

The smile in Sam's dark eyes dimmed a bit as he took a sip of his own beer before answering. "Wasn't easy at first," he admitted. "So many memories."

"Exactly." Cooper sighed with relief. Good to know he wasn't the only one wrestling with the images of the past. "Just sitting here, I can see us all clearly, playing over the line."

Sam smiled sadly as he, too, thought about those days. "You remember when Mac hit the home run through Gran's kitchen window?"

Cooper chuckled. "And it landed in her pot of spaghetti sauce? Who could forget?" The memories took hold of his throat and squeezed. To ease the tension, he added, "By the way, you should have had that ball."

"Right. It was miles out of my reach."

"Too lazy to jump for it," Cooper said, and took another sip of cold, frothy beer.

"Mac always could hit a ball like a bullet."

"Yeah." The beer suddenly tasted flat, bitter. "Damn it, Sam, I keep expecting to see him. Hear him."

"I did, too, at first," Sam said softly. "Then I realized Mac's gone. He's not here, Cooper. He's not hanging around trying to make us all feel bad about what happened."

"He doesn't have to," Cooper muttered and stood up, because he couldn't sit still another minute. Knots formed in his guts, his throat tightened and his mouth was suddenly dry. "God. Every day of my life I remember. And I feel bad. Guilty."

Sam looked up at him, understanding shining in his calm brown eyes. "There's no reason to."

"No reason? Mac *died.*" Cooper kicked at the dirt and watched pebbles skitter. "While we stood there like morons, Mac *died.*"

"We were kids, too," Sam reminded him and pushed his hair out of his eyes, when the wind blew it across his face.

"Yeah," Cooper said stiffly, "but we didn't die at sixteen."

And just like that, he was back there. On that long-ago summer day.

Playing one of their favorite games, the four cousins had lined up along the ridge above the ranch lake. One at a time, they ran and jumped in, while the guys on the bank timed them. You got points, not only for how far out you could jump, but for how long you stayed underwater.

Jake always won.

Mac though, had been determined to be the winner this time. He had outjumped Jake by a mile and Jake was seriously pissed. But to win, Mac had to stay underwater longer than he had, too.

Sam had the stopwatch and Cooper and Jake stood on either side of him while he timed Mac's turn. Jake got madder by the second, sure his best time was going to be beaten. Cooper hooted with glee that one of them had finally taken Jake down.

When Mac was underwater two minutes though, Sam started worrying. Wanted to go in after him. Cooper urged him to give Mac a few more seconds. Make sure Jake lost for a change.

And God, even now, Cooper could feel the wind in his face, the sun on his back. He heard Jake's muttered cursing and the note of worry in Sam's voice. Most of all though, he heard himself saying, "Don't be such an old woman, Sam. Mac's fine. He'll come up in a second."

Except he never did.

The three of them had—at last—jumped into the icy water after Mac and they'd found him. On the bottom of the lake. They'd dragged him out, tried mouth-to-mouth, but Mac was gone. The doctor said later he'd broken his neck in the fall and unconscious, had drowned.

And nothing since that day had ever been right again.

Cooper had avoided this ranch like the plague

ever since. Hell, they all had. Punishing themselves and each other. Now he was here again and damn it, he could hardly draw a breath without strangling on it.

Sam stood up and took a white-knuckled grip on his beer bottle. "Do you really think you have to remind me of what happened? Do you honestly believe that Mac's death hasn't chased me through the years as hard as it's chased you?"

In the cool shade of the old oak where they'd once played on a tire swing, Cooper stared at his cousin and saw the same torment in his eyes that he faced every morning in the mirror.

"No." He shook his head. "No, I don't. It's just..." he looked around, at the yard, the house, the barn, and felt the memories pulling at him as strong as a riptide. "I don't understand how you got past it. How you can live here and not choke on every breath?"

"I couldn't at first. Hell, I had my plans all laid out." He laughed shortly and took another drink of beer. "I was going to stay the summer, since Jeremiah had tricked me into giving my word—"

Cooper nodded wryly, since he, too, was caught by the same wily old man.

"—then," Sam continued, "I was going to hit the road again. Get as far from Coleville and the memories of Mac that I could."

"So what happened?" Cooper asked, then held up one hand. "Never mind. I know what happened."

He shot a glance at Maggie, now in a desperate tug-of-war with a golden retriever puppy over a wet pillowcase. "I like her, by the way."

Sam grinned. "Thanks. Me, too." His smile faded as he added, "It wasn't just falling in love with Maggie though. It was finding a way to make peace with Mac." His gaze locked on the woman he loved as she laughed, dropped to the ground and gathered the tiny dog to her chest. "Maggie helped me do that. Helped me see that Mac wouldn't want us torturing ourselves forever."

Cooper didn't know if he agreed with that or not, but he was willing to admit that the belief had certainly helped Sam. "Special woman."

"Beyond special," Sam said quietly. "She's everything."

Envy swept through Cooper again and was just as quickly brushed aside. After all, he wasn't interested in loving anybody. Too much risk came with love. Too high a chance at pain. And he'd already had enough pain to last a lifetime.

No. The only romance he was interested in, was the kind he wrote about. The kind he gave whatever hero and heroine he was dealing with in his latest book. And when he wrote their "happily ever after," his readers didn't know or care if he believed in it or not.

But unthinkingly, his gaze drifted to the edge of the field, where Kara walked with Jeremiah.

* * *

"It's good to have Cooper back home," Jeremiah said as he followed Kara's gaze to the two men standing beneath the oak tree at the far end of the yard.

"I can't believe he stayed away so long."

"They all had reason," he said on a sigh. "Or so they thought. Which amounts to the same thing, really."

Kara turned her gaze on the older man. His skin was leathery from a lifetime spent outdoors. Only a fringe of gray hair remained on his head, but his dark eyes, so much like Cooper's, sparkled with intensity.

She liked him a lot. Just as she liked Sam and Maggie. Kara had spent most of the afternoon trying not to be jealous of the other woman as she talked excitedly about her wedding plans and her pregnancy. In just a few weeks, Sam and Maggie would be getting married and moving into the main ranch house together.

Sam was taking over the local doctor's practice and Maggie was finishing school and…Kara's life felt emptier with every word Maggie had spoken. Terrible, she thought, immediately ashamed of herself. She should be happy for them. And she was. They seemed like perfectly nice people. But wasn't it only natural that she'd be just a little bit sorry for herself?

What did she have to show for her life?

A nicely balanced checkbook? A good apartment

and a tidy savings account? She was nearly thirty and beyond her mother, who made a point of calling at least once a week to remind her that she wasn't getting any younger, Kara had no one to care about. Or to care about her.

Something was definitely wrong with this picture.

She walked alongside Jeremiah, but only half listened as he talked about the ranch and what he and Sam were planning for it. Instead, her brain raced and though she didn't much like the decisions it was reaching, she had to admit that they were the right ones.

She'd put off quitting when she knew Cooper was having a hard time getting his latest book going. But she wasn't doing herself any favors by stretching this out. Better to just suck it up and make the move.

Her gaze shot to Cooper again, standing in the shade, laughing at something Sam had just said. And while her heart broke a little, she filled her mind with these pictures of him. Etched them into her brain so that years from now, she'd always be able to see him as he was today.

Then mentally, she started packing.

"Man, you're a great cook," Cooper said, leaning back in his chair at the kitchen table and grinning at Kara.

"Thanks, but steaks? They don't exactly require gourmet training."

"I've burned enough of 'em in my time to know that it takes a knack."

Kara shook her head. "Cooper, you are the only human being I know who could actually burn water."

"Sad, but true," he admitted and didn't look the least bit ashamed of himself. "I don't know what I'd do without you, Kara," he said and stood up to carry both plates to the sink. "Seriously," he went on when she didn't say anything, "you're the best."

"That's nice Cooper, but—"

He set the plates into the sink with a clatter. "You know though, you don't have to cook while we're here. You could hire someone locally to come in and do the cooking and cleaning."

All she had to do now was work up the nerve to tell him he was going to need not only a cook and a maid—but a new assistant. "Now that you mention it—"

A knock on the back door interrupted Kara and Cooper paused in clearing the table to go and open it. His grandfather stood on the porch, holding a foil covered plate.

Cooper grinned at the older man. "Didn't we just see you a few hours ago?"

"Sure did," Jeremiah said and pushed past his grandson without waiting for an invitation. Right on his heels came the puppy, its claws scrambling for traction on the old wood floor. It shot across the room, then put on the brakes and slid into the underside of the cabinet.

Jeremiah chuckled. "Told Maggie I'd take Sheba there for a walk and she loaded me down with a plate of her chocolate chip cookies to bring you two."

"Cookies? Always welcome," Cooper said, already reaching for the plate. "Oh, you can come in too, Jeremiah."

The older man laughed and stepped inside, taking a seat at the kitchen table. He reached out to pat Kara's hand and whispered, "Don't suppose you could spare an old man a cup of coffee? Maggie's got me drinking that decaffeinated stuff at night. Like to kill me."

"You bet," Kara said, pathetically grateful for the interruption and the chance to stall a few more minutes. *Why* couldn't she tell Cooper she was quitting? *Why* couldn't she bring herself to leave him? It was the right thing to do and she knew it. So why was it so hard?

In a few seconds, Cooper had the rest of the table cleared and Kara poured three cups of coffee.

The puppy lay under the table, contentedly chewing on the laces of Cooper's sneakers.

"So," Jeremiah said after a hearty sigh with his first sip of coffee, "you two see any ghosts yet?"

Cooper laughed and took a cookie for himself. "Haven't seen anything, but did hear something last night. Crying."

"More like sobbing," Kara corrected and cradled her own cup of coffee between her palms as if to ward off a chill she knew was coming.

"Yeah?"

Cooper laughed at his grandfather's eager expression. "Don't get excited. It's more likely somebody's playing a trick on us than it is for there to be a ghost in this house."

"Hell, boy," Jeremiah scoffed, "you write scary stories for a living and you don't believe in ghosts?"

Cooper's expression hardened. "Not the kind who make noises in old houses."

Kara watched as Cooper, in a heartbeat, distanced himself, even though he hadn't budged from his chair. It was as if he'd taken an emotional step back and she was clueless about what had caused it. But as she always did, she stepped in to help him out.

"Do you know anything about this house?" Kara asked, dissolving the taut silence and shifting his grandfather's attention from Cooper to her.

The older man sighed heavily, then gave her a small smile, as if to say he knew she was trying to smooth things over and he appreciated it. He gave her hand another friendly pat, took a sip of his coffee and said, "Everyone around here knows the story of this old house."

Cooper didn't say a word, so Kara urged, "Tell me."

Jeremiah nodded. "It was back during the gold rush era," he said, his deep voice slipping into storytelling mode as if he were born to it.

As he painted a vivid picture of the times, Kara

realized that Cooper had inherited his gift with words from his grandfather.

"Weren't many ranches here then. Most of the land was still owned by Spanish dons who weren't real happy about the yankees streaming into California by the boatload." He looked around the kitchen, took a sip of coffee and continued. "This house was built by one of the first to find gold. Bought the land from the local don, built this place and brought his wife out from back east. They had one daughter and when he died, he left the house to her—who, as young women will, fell in love with a scoundrel of a man."

"Oh, this doesn't have a happy ending, does it?" Kara murmured.

"If it did, it wouldn't be a ghost story, now would it?" Cooper took a drink of coffee and leaned back in his chair, his gaze fixed on his grandfather, sitting across from him.

Jeremiah ignored him and focused instead on Kara. "Oh, the young man loved her, but he was ambitious. He wanted to make his fortune more than he wanted to settle down. He left for the gold fields, promising to come back for her."

"He didn't?" Kara's heart hurt for the long-dead woman.

"She waited here for him," Jeremiah said, "for two long, lonely years. Desolate, she stood at the parlor window, crying for her lost love while she watched the road, hoping for a sign of him."

Pain swelled inside Kara and she could almost feel that poor woman's misery shivering in the air around her. Outside, the wind kicked up, spattering the window panes with dust and pebbles. A frigid puff of air scuttled through the kitchen and beneath the table, little Sheba growled, low in her throat.

"She died," Jeremiah said softly, almost reverently, "of a broken heart."

Cooper snorted.

Kara glared at him.

Jeremiah ignored him completely. "Without the love of her life, she simply couldn't go on."

Kara felt, rather than heard, a sigh.

"Every tenant since then never stays long in this place. It's not a happy house. Shame, really," Jeremiah said.

"What happened to her young man?"

The older man looked at her. "He finally did come for her, a few weeks after she died. But he was too late."

A shutter slapped against the side of the house and Kara jumped, startled.

Cooper laughed. "God, Kara, you should see your face. Jeremiah really got you going on that story, didn't he?"

His grandfather scowled at him, gray brows beetling. "Boy," he growled, sounding a lot like the puppy still restive beneath the table, "don't you think love is worth dying for?"

Cooper shook his head, got up and went for the coffeepot over on the counter. He refilled everyone's cup, then returned the pot before answering. "Jeremiah, the moral to that story is simple. Love isn't worth it."

"You got it all wrong, Coop," his grandfather said with a slow shake of his head. "Love is the only worthwhile thing there is."

Kara's heart sunk as she listened to the two men argue over the value of love. Emptiness opened up inside her and she felt a cold that went down deep into her bones. Her instincts had been right. Cooper would never love her. Never see her as anything more than an uber-efficient assistant and a pretty good cook.

It didn't matter how long she put off her decision, nothing was going to change. So what was the point of hanging around and torturing herself?

None.

An hour later, Jeremiah and the puppy were gone and the two of them were alone in the kitchen again. Working together, Kara dried the dishes as Cooper washed them. The silence was companionable, the task ordinary, and she knew there would never be a better time to say what she had to say.

"Cooper?"

"Yeah?" He turned to hand her another plate.

"I quit."

Five

"Very funny." Cooper gave her the plate and chuckling, turned back to the dirty dishes. "But don't joke about stuff like that."

"I'm not joking, Cooper."

"You'd better be, because you can't quit."

"Yes, I can. I just did. Consider this my two weeks' notice."

Cooper shut off the water and turned to face her. Her dark brown hair was pulled back from her face and held by one of those clip things that opened like an alligator's jaws. In the overhead light, her big green eyes were shadowed as she looked at him, and there wasn't so much as a hint of a smile on her face.

A solitary thread of worry slithered through him.

"Is this about the ghost thing? And the crying last night? Because if it is, don't worry about it—I swear it's just somebody playing a dumb joke."

"It's not about the crying, or the ghost story. It's about us."

Now he was really confused. "*Us?* What about us?"

She tossed the yellow-and-white striped dish-towel onto the counter, then folded her arms under her breasts, tipped her head to one side and glared at him. "You don't get it at all, do you?"

"Apparently not."

"So typical."

"What'd I do?"

She unfolded her arms, slapped her hands on her hips and said, "Nothing. Ever. Just nothing." Before he could speak, she held up one hand for silence, took a deep breath and said shortly, "Never mind. Let's just say that I'm quitting because we can't keep going on like this."

"Like what?" Why did he suddenly feel like he was speaking Greek in a Chinese restaurant?

"Like we are, Cooper."

"What's wrong with it?" And why was she suddenly not making any sense to him at all?

"It's like we're married, Cooper. Only without any of the good stuff. Like sex."

Instantly, the memory of her in that pretty silk nightie popped into his brain and set fire to a completely different part of his anatomy. He had to admit that up until the night before, he'd never really thought about Kara and sex in the same sentence. But now, he wasn't so sure. "You want us to have sex?"

Kara blew out a frustrated breath, reached up and tugged the clip from her hair then shook her head and rubbed at the spot where it had been. All of that thick, dark brown hair flew about her face in soft waves and made Cooper want to reach out and comb his fingers through it.

Hey, maybe sex was a good idea.

"Of course I want sex. But I want more than that, too." Sighing, she said, "I want a husband. Kids. A home. I've been working for you for five years and all I've got to show for it is a nice savings account and a few new recipes."

"So you've been miserable working for me? Is that it?"

"No, that's not it at all. Just the opposite, in fact," she said irritably. "I got so comfortable that I didn't notice that I wasn't getting anywhere."

"What's so bad about comfortable?" he demanded, suddenly realizing that she might just be serious about quitting. Her eyes shone with regret, but there was no going back with Kara. He knew that already. Once she'd made up her mind about something, that was it.

And the thought of losing Kara hit him hard.

"Nothing," she said, "if that's all you're looking

for, then comfortable is great. But it's not enough for me. Not anymore."

"Hold on," he countered, feeling his heart jolt in his chest. "This is all coming out of the blue for me, Kara. As far as I knew, everything between us was working great."

"Well sure," she snapped, throwing both hands high and letting them slap to her sides again. "Why wouldn't it be great from your point of view? I take care of everything for you. I pay your bills, talk to your editors, handle your publicity, pick up your dry cleaning…you can't even make a decent pot of coffee on your own."

"Hey!" Insulted, and not just because most of what she said was true, Cooper stared at her like he'd never seen her before. In the five years they'd been together, Kara had always been calm, cool, reasonable. This Kara had sparks flying from her eyes.

Which he was just twisted enough to actually think sexy.

"It's not entirely your fault," she conceded. "God knows, I worked hard at making myself indispensable."

"Did a good job of it, too." Cooper tried a smile out on her and felt a quick stab of disappointment when it didn't warm her eyes. "How about a raise? Would that make you feel differently?"

"No!" Frustration ringing in her voice, she said loudly, "It's not about the money, Cooper. It never was."

He reached for her, but she took a quick half step back. "Kara, you can't quit. I need you too much."

"That's exactly why I have to go!" She inhaled sharply, deeply and blew the air out again in a rush. "Don't you get it? If I keep acting like your wife, I'll never get to really *be* one."

Those sparks in her eyes were flashing like warning lights at the edge of a cliff. And Cooper was bright enough to back off fast. "You're tired. Why don't you sleep on it and we can talk about this in the morning when you're calmer?"

"Grrrrrr..." Kara tugged at her hair again and shouted, "I'm perfectly calm."

"Yeah," he assured her, keeping a wary distance between them. "I can see that."

"Honestly Cooper, you can be the most infuriating man..." She turned on her heel, stomped across the kitchen and marched into the living room. Just before she turned for the stairs, she stopped dead, turned her head and fried him with a look. "Just so you know. I'm not going to change my mind. I *am* quitting."

Then she stomped up the stairs, managing to sound like an invading army, which just proved to Cooper that she was too upset to be making major decisions. He walked to the doorway and winced when she slammed her bedroom door. She'd feel differently in the morning.

He could talk his way around Kara.

She'd see reason.

So why, he wondered, was he suddenly so worried?

When the sobbing started in the middle of the night, Kara was already awake. The muffled crying seemed to weep from the walls, surrounding her in a sea of pain that was strong enough to bridge the centuries. Cold crept through the bedroom and sighed around Kara.

Despite what Cooper might like to think, this was no joke. And Kara knew she should be terrified. Should be running screaming from the old house, putting as much distance between her and the ghost as she possibly could. But she didn't feel *fear.* She felt…compassion.

Sitting up in bed, she rubbed her bare arms as tears welled up in her eyes. Empathy for the long-dead woman filled her and Kara realized that she and the ghost had a lot in common.

Okay, not *a lot.*

After all, Kara was still alive.

But the ghost had waited for love until it was too late—Kara had waited, too, hoping that Cooper would see how good they could be together. The sobbing woman had allowed the longing for love to kill her. Kara wouldn't make the same mistake.

"I'm so sorry," she whispered, glancing around the shadow-filled room as tears rolled unheeded down her cheeks. "I'm sorry for both of us."

* * *

Cooper, wide awake and trying to work, jolted as the sobbing began. Already, he was on edge since he hadn't been able to write a single coherent sentence since Kara had told him she quit. All he could think about was her. And how in the hell he could convince her to change that stubborn mind of hers.

The crying was just what he needed as a distraction. He jumped up and headed for his bedroom door. Yanking it open, he stepped into the hall and paused, waiting for Kara to appear as she had the night before. In his mind, he saw her again, hair tumbled about her face, that silky nightgown and all of her bare, tanned skin. But her door didn't open. Did she not hear the crying? Unlikely. She was simply trying to avoid him. That simple truth jabbed at him and he scowled at her closed door. Damn it, how could she quit? How could she walk away from him?

Cooper muttered darkly, then headed down the hall alone, following the crying as it seemed to float through the house. He didn't care what Jeremiah said, Cooper didn't believe in ghosts and he was going to find the damn joker behind these nightly visits.

He didn't bother with turning on the lights, finding his way with no problem, since moonlight filtered through the windows. The wood floor cool beneath his bare feet, Cooper moved soundlessly through the house, determined to put an end to this ghost stuff once and for all.

Only last night, he thought, he and Kara had been in this together. And a part of him missed having her with him. Missed the feel of her hand in his as they slipped through the shadows. Missed the sense of…teamwork, they'd always shared.

Damn. How could she *quit?*

Pushing that furious thought out of his head, he concentrated instead on the mournful cries reverberating around him. The night before, when Kara had been with him, the sobs had led them to the parlor. Tonight, the terrible crying took him to the front door.

Smirking to himself, he muttered, "Trick me into opening the front door? Bet Mike Haney's crouched on the porch laughing himself sick over this."

Grabbing the brass doorknob, Cooper threw the door open, expecting to come face-to-face with some practical joker.

But no one was there.

He took a step forward and stopped dead.

A wall of icy cold blocked the doorway.

Cooper sucked in air like a drowning man. His heartbeat jumped into a frantic beat that felt as though it was going to burst through his chest. Chills snaked along his spine. His throat squeezed shut and his mouth went dry.

The cold was immovable. Solid. As if it had always been there.

Around him, the sobs grew harsher, louder, more desperate.

Moonlight spilled onto the lawn, spearing through the trees, laying down lacy patterns that dipped and swayed in the wind.

"Mike Haney's not behind *this*," he whispered, scrubbing one hand across his face as his heartbeat slowly returned to normal.

This was no joke. The wall of cold was too real to be ignored or explained. He watched as his breath formed tiny clouds of mist in front of his face. Nope. No joke. This was yet another ghost.

The too late lover?

The cold pressed forward, trying to enter. Trying to get into the house, even if it had to go through Cooper. He felt the pressure against his chest as if someone were pushing him. The small hairs at the back of his neck stood straight up as the sobbing in the house became a moaning wail and then nearly a shriek of desperation fueled by fury.

It was one thing to *write* about ghosts. It was totally another to actually *live* with one.

"Is that what this is all about?" he asked, not really expecting an answer. "She's been waiting for you and you're finally trying to get into the house?"

His breath misted. Chills raced up and down his spine, but he fought off the instinct to close the door. If he could solve this ghost problem, maybe the long-dead lady would stop crying in the night. So instead, he opened it wider, stood back and waved one arm in silent invitation. "Come on then. Come find your woman and apologize or whatever it is you're trying to do and—"

The door was snatched free of his grip and slammed closed with a force that rattled the window panes.

Cooper blew out a breath and looked around the suddenly silent room. The cold was locked outside, the crying ghost was quiet—and apparently pissed off—and he was just as confused as ever. According to Jeremiah, this ghost had been waiting for her lover for a hundred and fifty years. Now that he's come she won't let him in?

Women.

"He's the most stubborn man on the face of the planet," Kara said grimly and snapped a green bean neatly in half.

"Believe me," Maggie said with a quiet smile. "I totally understand."

"No, you couldn't possibly." Kara pushed up from the table set under the oak tree in the backyard of Cooper's grandfather's ranch. She'd come to talk to Maggie, Sam's fiancée, because frankly, she was going a little stir crazy.

The last few days had crawled past.

Cooper wouldn't talk to her. Wouldn't even *acknowledge* the fact that she'd quit her job. Whenever she tried to talk to him about arranging for a temp until he could find someone permanent, he only gave her a patient smile. He wasn't listening. Wasn't taking her seriously.

Heck, she was going to have to actually leave to convince him she meant business.

"Trust me," Maggie said as she leaned back in her chair and stretched her legs out in front of her. "I think stubborn is a Lonergan family trait."

Kara shook her hair back out of her face as a quick wind kicked up out of nowhere, carrying on it the scent of the sea. She took a deep breath, blew it out and made a concentrated effort to calm herself.

It didn't work.

Lifting one hand, she rubbed her aching eyes. The headache that had been creeping up on her for hours was now in full bloom and every muscle in her body hurt. It was lack of sleep, she knew. Had to be.

The ghost had been in fine voice the last three nights. And every night, Kara sat in her room alone, listening to a long-dead woman cry for her lost love. It was as if the ghost were trying to tell Kara something. Warn her. *Don't let this happen to you,* she seemed to be saying.

"Are you okay?"

Turning around to look at the other woman, Kara swallowed hard, forced a smile she didn't feel and said, "Yes. I'm fine. Just…tired."

"The ghost?"

Kara smiled again. "You don't have any trouble believing?"

"No." Maggie stood up and walked to Kara's side. Dappled shade from the tree swept across her face in a lacy pattern. "Love's the strongest emotion there is. Why shouldn't it be able to linger long after we've gone?"

"I feel so bad for her," Kara said, "it's not just hearing her. I can feel her pain. Her sorrow is so profound, so all encompassing that—" What? That she was beginning to think the ghost was trying to communicate with her? Kara shook her head at her own crazy thoughts and chuckled. "Though I could really use some sleep."

"You sure you're only tired?" Maggie's dark gaze fixed on her with concern. "You sort of look feverish. I could take you into town, have Sam give you a checkup."

Kara's stomach turned and she sucked in a gulp of air to steady it. She didn't want to see a doctor. She just wanted to go. To leave Coleville and Cooper behind so she could start the big plan of getting over him.

"Honest. I'm fine." She tried another smile and added, "I actually came over here to ask you for a favor, Maggie."

"Sure, what is it?"

"I told you that Cooper won't admit that I quit my job?"

"Uh-huh."

"Well, I've decided the only way to prove it to him is to just go."

"You're leaving?"

"I have to," she said firmly, not really sure if she was trying to convince Maggie, or herself. But did it matter? "I wanted to give him two weeks' notice, but he's not listening to me, so what's the point? Anyway, until I can arrange for a temporary assistant for him, Cooper's going to be on his own—and he'll probably starve if someone doesn't remind him to eat occasionally."

"You're worried about him."

"Only natural," Kara said, trying to shrug off Maggie's words. "I've been running his world for five years. Without me, he's going to be lost." Just as she would be without him. "So I was wondering if you'd mind checking up on him once in awhile. You know, just…make sure he goes grocery shopping for more than frozen burritos?"

Maggie watched her for several long seconds and Kara wanted to squirm under the woman's steady regard. Finally though, Maggie said, "I'll be happy to—if you answer one question for me."

Kara sighed. "What is it?"

"Why don't you tell Cooper that you're in love with him?"

Surprised, Kara thought briefly about denying the truth. Then, looking into Maggie's understanding gaze, she figured, why bother? Rubbing at her forehead again in an attempt to quiet the pounding just behind her eyes, she said softly, "Because he doesn't want to know."

"But loving him, can you really walk away?" Maggie asked, reaching out to lay one hand on Kara's forearm.

"I have to," she said, wishing things were different. "While I still can."

Cooper was waiting for her.

Twilight filled the kitchen. Candles on the old table stood straight and tall, their flames dipping and swaying in the breeze. From the living room came the quiet, smooth sound of old jazz playing on the stereo. Everything was set. He had dinner made—even he could make pasta—and a bottle of wine open and breathing on the table.

Over the last few days, he'd done a lot of thinking—mostly because he hadn't been able to do anything else. He couldn't concentrate enough to write and couldn't talk to Kara without her talking about leaving him. This afternoon, he'd decided on a plan of action.

She walked inside, closed the door, then turned to face him.

Cooper looked her over, head to toe. Her dark brown hair had been tossed by the wind and her green eyes glittered in the reflected sunlight. She wore denim shorts, a pale yellow tank top and white sandals. She looked…*beautiful*.

Why had he never really noticed before? When had he become the kind of man who didn't pay attention to the people around him? Had he really become so secluded that he didn't even take notice of the woman who kept his entire life running on schedule?

"What's wrong?" she asked.

"What?"

"What's wrong, Cooper?"

"Nothing." He shook his head, told himself to quit with the self-analysis and get down to the plan. "Nothing's wrong."

"Good." She sniffed the air. "You *cooked?*"

"Contrary to popular belief, I'm not a complete moron."

"Pasta?" she asked, giving him a half smile.

"With chicken this time."

"Ah, innovation." She smiled a bit, then asked, "What's this about?"

He stepped up close and laid both hands on her shoulders. She looked up into his eyes and something inside Cooper clicked. He didn't know what the hell it was, but it was there and it was…important.

Don't think about it now, he told himself.

"What're you doing, Cooper?"

"I've been thinking."

She gave him a half smile. "I'll alert the media."

"Ha-ha." He pulled her closer and enjoyed the hell out of the look of surprise that flickered in her eyes. "I think I figured out what the problem is between us—"

She huffed out a breath. "You mean the problem where I quit and you don't believe me?"

"No, the other one."

"There's another one? This should be good."

"I think so."

"Okay, tell me," she said, squirming a little in an attempt to either get closer or move away—he wasn't entirely sure which.

"It's unrelieved sexual tension, Kara," he murmured, his gaze moving over her face before settling briefly on her mouth, her full bottom lip and that top lip that she always chewed on when she was worried about something.

Like she was doing now.

He smiled. "Why don't you let me chew on that lip for you?"

She went perfectly still and blinked up at him. "Are you *serious?*"

He pulled her hips tight against him so she could feel just how serious he really was. Her green eyes went wide and she huffed in a quick breath. His gaze dropped to the swell of her breasts, barely visible over the edge of her tank top.

A rush of need, much stronger, hotter, deeper than he'd expected, pumped through him and he drew her even closer, dipping his head to hers. She fit perfectly against him and he wondered why he'd never noticed that, either. And wondered why the hell it had taken him so long to come up with this plan.

She wanted him, he could see it in her eyes. He wanted her too. So what could be simpler than having each other? And once they'd had sex, she'd quit talking about leaving and things could go back to normal.

Brilliant.

"Well?" He lifted one hand to smooth her hair back from her face, then trailed his fingertips along the line of her jaw. She shivered and he smiled. "What do you say we get rid of all this tension?"

"I should warn you, I'm feeling pretty tense," she said, slowly sliding her hands up his chest until she could hook her arms around his neck. "This could take awhile."

He smiled and brushed his mouth against hers, once, twice, experiencing a surprising jolt of something hot and amazing each time. Then he met her gaze and promised, "Work, work, work."

Six

Kara's head was spinning, the headache behind her eyes was pounding and even her stomach wasn't very happy.

But all of that paled into nothingness the minute Cooper's mouth came down on hers. It was everything she'd been dreaming about…and so much more.

She sighed into him and gave herself up to the spiraling sensations unwinding inside her. He parted her lips with his tongue and she gasped at the sensual invasion. Their tongues met in an erotic dance that began smoothly, softly and quickly escalated into erupting need.

His arms came around her waist and he held her

tightly to him. So tightly, she felt his erection against her abdomen and her muscles quivered in anticipation. She'd wanted this, needed this for so very long, she could hardly believe it was finally happening.

Maybe she shouldn't give into the urges clamoring inside her. Maybe she should back up, step out of his arms, end this moment of fantasy. But the instant that thought raced through her brain, she greedily shut it down.

He slid one of his hands up her spine to cup the back of her head, fingers spearing through her hair. She moaned and leaned into him, taking more, giving more.

One corner of her brain screamed at her to be logical. Rational. To *think* for heaven's sake.

But she didn't want to think.

Not anymore.

Now, all she wanted, was to *feel*.

It didn't matter that she was a little woozy, that her headache had already begun slipping back up on her or that her stomach was none too steady.

If she had *bubonic plague*, she wouldn't have been too sick to have sex with Cooper. Not after she'd spent so much time over the last year imagining it, dreaming about it.

And oh boy, so far, it was *way* better than her dreams.

He tore his mouth from hers and dropped his head to the curve of her neck. His teeth and tongue slid over her flesh, sending ripples of something hot and delicious crashing through her.

His breath hot on her skin, his voice came muffled, strained. "Dinner can wait. Let's go upstairs."

Upstairs.

To a bed.

Oh, boy.

Once he stood back from her and took her hand to lead her from the kitchen, Kara's brain woke up with a new set of warning signals. *You're planning to leave. You've already quit. Is this really the right thing to do? Won't this only make it even harder for you to live without him?*

Probably, she acknowledged to the voice in her brain she was seriously starting to hate. But loving him, could she really not take the opportunity to have him for herself? If only for one night?

Not a chance.

He hit the stairs at a dead run and pulled her along in his wake. Kara stumbled a bit, but kept up, her much shorter legs having to move twice as fast. At the landing, he made a sharp right turn to his bedroom and when he'd pulled her in behind him, he slammed the door, enclosing them both in the big room.

A soft breeze rippled the curtains over the windows and the spicy scent of geraniums, mingled with the richer scent of summer roses, filled the air. She hardly noticed. All Kara knew was that Cooper was looking at her as she'd always wanted him to and nothing else mattered.

His dark eyes shone with a fire Kara had never seen before and it was all for her. It didn't matter that he didn't feel for her what she did for him. Not at the moment anyway. All that mattered now was this minute. This room. This man.

Cooper reached for the hem of her pale yellow tank top and in one smooth, practiced move, pulled it up and over her head before tossing it onto the floor.

"Gorgeous," he murmured and as Kara swayed unsteadily, he undid the front clasp of her bra and pushed it off her shoulders. His hands cupped her breasts and when his thumbs and forefingers tweaked her nipples, Kara heard a groan and only belatedly realized it had come from her.

Abruptly, his hands dropped to her waist. He scooped her up, tossed her onto the bed, then stood looking down at her with a smile. "Can't think why we never did this before, Kara."

"Me neither," she said, lifting both arms in welcome.

He grinned, reached down and pulled her denim shorts off, then paused a second or two to admire her white lace thong. "Man, if I'd known you were wearing something like that under your sensible clothes, I swear, it wouldn't have taken me five years to see it."

That nagging ache behind her eyes dulled a bit as she enjoyed the rush of his admiration.

She'd wanted this so long, hoped for it, dreamed

about it, that she wanted to remember every second. Every feeling. Every image. She wanted to imprint on her brain the sensation of Cooper's hands on her skin. She wanted to commit to memory the rough sound of his voice and the hot flash in his eyes.

Oh, she wanted it all.

For one night, she wanted it all.

Delicately, Cooper slid his fingers beneath the fragile elastic band of her thong and slowly, sensually, slid it off, caressing her thighs, her calves, as he went.

Kara chewed at her top lip and shifted impatiently on the quilt covered mattress. She watched him with hungry eyes as he quickly tore his own clothes off and then loomed over her on the bed.

He was simply amazing.

Body sculpted by the gods, his skin was bronzed, and her fingers itched to caress him. Reaching up, she smoothed her palms across his chest and over his shoulders and he sucked in a breath through gritted teeth at her touch. Then he dipped his head and took first one of her hardened nipples into his mouth and then the other.

Dizzying sensations rocked her and she held onto him as if it meant her life. Arching into him, she sighed breathlessly as his mouth worked her flesh into a tingling mass of nerves. His hands kept moving, sweeping up and down the length of her body, exploring, caressing, stroking. Wave after wave of desire crashed inside her, leaving Kara a whimpering mass of need.

Cooper shifted over her, raising his head just enough to kiss her, to take her mouth with a hunger that matched her own. His left hand dropped to her center and his fingertips slid across her damp folds, sliding back and forth with a sure, tender touch that spiked her desire into a frenzy.

Rocking her hips into his hand, she sighed into his mouth as he dipped his fingers deep within her. He used first one, then two fingers, to tantalize her, to push her to the very brink of climax—only to pull her back, demanding she stay hungry.

"Cooper," she whispered, tearing her mouth from his long enough to snatch at desperately needed air. "Cooper, I need…"

"So do I, Kara," he murmured, looking down into her eyes. His breath came in short, sharp gulps as he watched anticipation crest and recede on her features. "Let me watch you go over."

"No," she said, twisting her head from side to side, and smiling, though it cost her. "No, I want you. Inside me. Now. Now, Cooper."

"You're killing me, Kara," he said, dipping his head long enough to steal a kiss and taste her need.

She managed a short laugh, then lifted both hands to cup his face, even as his thumb brushed across a most sensitive nub at her center. "Oh, not yet. Definitely, not yet."

He swallowed hard and pulled away from her. Kara wanted to drag him back instantly, but she watched him reach over to the bedside table and yank open the drawer. He pulled a box of condoms out, then tore the package apart, grabbed one foil packet and quickly took care of the necessities of sex in the twenty-first century.

In seconds, he was back, touching her, stroking her, moving to position himself between her thighs. She moved with him, eager now to feel him inside her. To feel him take her deep and fast and hard.

While his fingers worked that one tender bud, he pushed his body into hers, and Kara gasped as she stretched to accommodate him. Her body awakened in a series of sparkling jolts of awareness. He rocked his hips against hers, pushing deeper with every thrust.

"Cooper…" She tipped her head back, into the mattress, closed her eyes and concentrated solely on the amazing sensations peaking inside her. She smiled, gasped and smiled again. "So…good. So…good."

"Let go, Kara," he said, pushing himself deeper into her body, shuddering with the force of his own all encompassing need. For the first time in his life, Cooper felt connected to the act of sex. To the wonder of it. To the incredible sense of expectation crowding at the edges of his brain.

He fought for control—despite knowing he wouldn't find it. He'd never before so lost himself in the moment. Never experienced this rush of tenderness and passion so completely commingled before.

And staring down into Kara's passion glazed green eyes, he knew that nothing would ever be simple between them again. Yet he couldn't bring himself to care.

He needed to hold her closer, deeper. To feel himself sliding so deeply within her that they would be locked together. Groaning, he leaned back, sitting on his heels and drawing Kara up with him, until she was on his lap, legs at either side of him, impaled on his body.

Her head fell back as she held onto his shoulders. His hands at her hips, he lifted her, moving her up and down on his body, drawing her up and down his length until neither of them could breathe. Until the passion was so thick in the room they were strangling on it.

He felt it when her climax rushed in. Knew the exact instant when she finally released the tension within and rode the first wave of completion.

Her body arched and she swiveled her hips on him, taking him even deeper. "Cooper! It's too much!"

"It's not," he told her brokenly. "It's not too much."

The air around them seemed to sigh, echoing softly in a tender whisper.

Their eyes met and locked and Kara's fingers dug into his shoulders as she groaned, trembling against him.

And holding her tightly to him, Cooper at last allowed himself to follow. Then when the tremors eased and the electricity arcing between them shimmered to an end, Cooper rested his forehead on her shoulder and tried to keep his thundering heart in his chest where it belonged.

Seconds ticked past, with the only sound in the room, their labored breathing. Then long before Cooper was willing to move, Kara shifted in his grasp and murmured, "Uh-oh."

"Hmm?" He tightened his grip on her and felt his body stir again. Sucking in air, even he was surprised by just how quickly he needed her again.

"Cooper," she whispered, "let me go."

"Not yet." He lifted his head, looked into her eyes and gave her a smile. "I kind of like you just where you are."

She shook her head, and inhaled sharply through her nose. "I need to—"

"Hey, I need something too and—"

"*No.*" Eyes suddenly wild, she clambered off his lap, pushed off the bed and staggered hurriedly out of the bedroom to the bathroom off the hall. She slapped the door open and in seconds, Cooper heard her being violently ill.

Frowning now, Cooper followed her into the bathroom and stood in the open doorway. As the first bout of sickness left her gasping for air, leaning back against the edge of the tub, he said, "You know, if this is a comment on my lovemaking skills, I want you to know I've never had this particular complaint before."

Clearly miserable, Kara swept her hair back out of her face and muttered thickly, "Go away, Cooper."

"Are you okay?" he asked, going down on one knee.

"*No* would be the short answer," she said, then gulped, "oh, no…"

Kara gripped the edges of the toilet and wished she could just open a hole to the center of the Earth and fall into it. How could her world go from glorious to miserable in the space of a couple minutes? And oh, *why* did she have to be so sick in front of Cooper?

"Take it easy," he whispered from just behind her. He held her hair back and soothed her with muttered nonsense as she turned inside out.

When she could take a breath, she tried again. "Cooper, if you care anything about me at all, you'll go away. Leave me to my misery in private."

He actually had the nerve to chuckle. Vaguely, she heard water running in the sink and then he was back, holding a cool damp cloth to her forehead while she was sick. And when she was at last finished, wanting only to curl up on the deliciously cold bathroom floor, he scooped her up in his arms and carried her back to the bedroom and to his bed.

Head pounding, mouth feeling like she'd been

sipping a sewer and a raceway for goose bumps forming on her spine, Kara wished absently that she were alive enough to enjoy being carried. But at the moment, that was simply beyond her.

She did try one more time to slink back to her own room. "Cooper, I just need to sleep," she said, trying to push up from the mattress on arms that suddenly felt too weak to support her.

"And you're going to," he said, helping her into a bathrobe and pulling the quilt out from under her, then draping it across her still form and tucking it tenderly in.

Damn it, he was being *nice*. And she was too weak and humiliated to protest. Apparently, the Fates had quite a sense of humor—and the joke was on her. She'd wanted him forever and it wasn't until *now* he paid attention. Now when she finally gets him into bed, she has to end the interlude by worshipping at the porcelain altar.

God.

Maybe she was weak enough to die.

"You're burning up," Cooper said, resting his hand on her forehead briefly.

"No I'm not," she argued, "I'm *freezing*." She burrowed deeper under the quilt and made a conscious effort to keep her teeth from chattering.

"Right. Okay. Stay put. I'm gonna call Sam."

"Sam?" She shook her head and looked up at him. He stood there beside the bed in all his naked glory and Kara couldn't even bring herself to care. She really was sick.

"He's a doctor. He'll know what to do."

"I don't need a doctor. Mortician, maybe."

"Funny." He grabbed his jeans off the floor and tugged them on, not bothering with the button fly. He scraped one hand through his hair and headed for the door. "I'll be back."

An hour later, Sam and Cooper stood in the kitchen. The candles he'd had burning when Kara came home had long since guttered out in their own wax puddles. The pasta was cold and congealed in a bowl on the table and the lingering scent of garlic still seasoned the air.

"You're sure she's okay?"

"Trust me," Sam said, snapping his black leather bag closed. "It's the flu. Kara will be fine in a couple of days. Just make sure she rests and gets lots of fluids."

"That's it?" Cooper demanded, glaring at his cousin. "You go to medical school for God knows how many years and the best you can do is *take a nap*?"

"Hey, you called me for my professional opinion, remember?"

"Right." Cooper blew out a breath. He didn't like this. He liked Kara up and annoying him. Ordering him around. Seeing her so weak and tired and…sick, worried him. "So should she eat anything?"

"Not till tomorrow at least. Then light stuff. Chicken soup, crackers." Sam studied him for a minute or two, then shook his head. "I can arrange for a nurse to come in and take care of her if you want."

Cooper's gaze snapped to his. "No. I'll do it."

"You sure?" Sam's voice was disbelieving and who could blame him?

Cooper couldn't remember a single time in his life when he'd voluntarily put himself out for someone else. Man. What did that say about him?

That he was a miserable, selfish jerk. Which he already knew. Hell, since that summer fifteen years ago, he'd done his best to keep a safe distance between himself and the human race. It had started deliberately. He even remembered making the choice to pull back, not only from his cousins, but from his parents, his grandfather, his friends.

Then after a few years, that distance had become a part of him. A part of his life that he'd grown so comfortable with, he'd never tried to change. Safer that way. Easier.

Until now.

But this was different.

This was Kara.

"It's not rocket science, Sam," he snapped, shoving both hands into his jeans pockets and rocking on his heels. "I can take care of the house and one sick woman."

"Okay," Sam nodded, eyeing him speculatively,

as if he wasn't quite sure Cooper meant what he was saying. Then he shrugged. "Maggie will probably want to come over tomorrow to check on her anyway, though."

"She doesn't have to, but thanks."

"Now, I'm going home." Sam turned for the back door, opened it, then stopped, looking at Cooper over his shoulder. "And while you're at it, you ought to get some rest, too. You look like hell."

Cooper shrugged off Sam's suggestion and once his cousin was gone, set the teakettle on the antique stove and turned on the burner. Rummaging through the kitchen cabinets, he located a coffee mug, then finally unearthed the jasmine tea bags that Kara had bought her first day in town.

Hitching one hip against the counter, he stared at the kitchen windows and the night crouched just beyond the circle of lamplight. He caught his own reflection in the glass and admitted that Sam had a point. He *did* look like hell. Worry etched itself into his eyes and bracketed his mouth.

Not too surprising. Of *course* he was worried about Kara. She was a part of his life. And tonight, she'd become an even bigger part.

A draft of cold air slipped past him and he shivered. Still staring at the glass, while the water in the teakettle began to stir, Cooper noticed a flash of movement. A white, shadowy film that moved across the glass and then disappeared.

He straightened up slowly and only absently heard the low pitch of the teakettle beginning to hum. He looked around the empty room and wasn't even surprised when he heard a heavy sigh reverberate around him.

The teakettle began shrieking, the sound driving into his head like a nail. He took the two steps to the stove, shut the fire off and flipped the cap off the kettle to end the noise. He poured a steaming stream of water into the cup, instantly releasing a flowery aroma.

While the tea steeped, he searched through the pantry for a couple of soda crackers. Despite what Sam had said, he figured Kara might be hungry and he wanted to be ready. When the tea was ready and the crackers on a small plate, he picked them up and looked around the room again.

"You still here?" Weird. Talking to a ghost. Weirder still, he was half expecting an answer. When nothing happened, he headed out to the stairs. At the door to his bedroom, he stopped. In the soft puddle of light from the bedside lamp, Kara lay, sound asleep.

He walked into the room, set the tea down on the dresser and placed the crackers alongside it. Then Cooper took a nearby armchair and dragged it to the side of the bed. He sat down and felt another cold chill brush along his shoulders and he stiffened reflexively.

Whispering into the quiet room, he said, "I'd appreciate it if you could skip the crying tonight. Kara's sick and she needs to sleep."

For several long moments, nothing happened, and then Cooper felt the chill in the room slide away, as if it had never been. Nodding to himself, he settled into the chair, got comfortable and prepared for a long night of keeping watch over Kara.

Seven

The cold was a living wall, surrounding him, devouring him. David felt it taking small bites of his heart, his soul. Helpless to stop it, he could only observe helplessly as the cold slowly, inexorably, eased into every corner of his being.

But there was something more, too. Something less substantial than the cold and yet far more insidious. Like an oil spill, it filled him, an inky blackness that was slowly obliterating who he had been before he'd first entered the hotel.

Worse, he couldn't fight it.

A scream slashed through the silence,

tearing it as a sharp blade would rend fragile
silk. And...and... Damn it.

"Then what?" Cooper said aloud as he flopped
back against the chair and glared at the screen of his
laptop computer as if the machine itself were deliberately sabotaging him. A scream? Who the hell
screamed? And why?

Usually, he worked through his books by the seat
of his pants, believing strongly that if he ever sat
down and plotted the thing out, scene by scene, he'd
suck the heart of it out. The immediacy. And besides,
he sort of enjoyed being surprised by whatever his
characters got into.

But now...he couldn't think. Couldn't concentrate on his book because he couldn't stop thinking
about the woman upstairs, lying in his bed. Sitting
in a chair in his bedroom, he'd managed to doze off
a couple times during the night. But every time Kara
moaned or sighed in her fevered sleep, she'd brought
him right out of it again.

His eyes felt like two marbles rolling in sand.
Lifting both hands, he rubbed them, making the ache
more pronounced. Then he braced his elbows on the
tabletop and cupped his face in his palms. How was
he supposed to come up with a fictional horror story
while he was so concerned about Kara? Should the
flu really be this hard on a person? Shouldn't she be
feeling better by now?

Kara wouldn't drink any of the tea he brought her. Turned green at the offering of soda crackers and only spoke to tell him to go away.

As a nurse, he was a bust.

Or maybe Sam was a quack and she needed something more than rest.

Pushing up from the chair at the kitchen table, he stalked out of the room, across the living room and up the stairs, his long legs taking them two at a time. He turned for his bedroom and knocked quietly before opening the door.

Kara turned her head on the pillow to look at him as he entered. In the sunlight, her skin was too pale and lavender shadows lay beneath her eyes. She looked exhausted.

"Cooper, at least let me go back to my own bed."

"No," he said, giving her a smile she didn't want. "You're not getting out of that bed until you can do it without racing to the bathroom."

She tugged the quilt up to her chin and sulked. "I'm not a child," she pointed out.

"I remember," he said.

She groaned and pulled the quilt up over her face. Voice muffled, she said, "Oh, God, don't."

"Don't what?"

"Remember." She weakly pushed the quilt back down but closed her eyes as if she couldn't bear to look at him. "Put the whole night out of your mind. I have."

That stung more than he would have thought

possible. Amazing how much difference a few hours could make. Last night, he'd held her in his arms, locked himself inside her body and felt her quickening response. Today…they were like two polite strangers.

The easy camaraderie they used to share was gone. Friendship splintered by sex. Sex she didn't even want to think about. Great. By changing their relationship, he'd hoped to convince her not to quit. Now, it was starting to look like he'd only accelerated the process. Hell, she was lying there in his bed and already further away from him than she'd ever been. Disgusted with himself and the situation, he said, "I'm going into town. Pick up a few supplies."

"Good. Go away."

"Won't be gone long," he said, paying no attention to her crabbiness. "I'm going to ask Maggie to come sit with you. Make sure you stay in that bed."

Her eyes opened so she could glare at him briefly. "I'm not an infant. I can survive on my own for a couple of hours."

He ignored her tone, figuring a person was allowed to be crabby when they felt like hell. He always did. And the last time he was sick, he remembered suddenly, Kara had been at his side the whole time. He'd never questioned it, never even really taken the time to *appreciate* it. *God, what an idiot.* "Trust me, I don't think of you as an infant. But Maggie'll be here anyway."

"I don't need a sitter. I just need to get well."

"You will."

"When?"

"Okay," he said smiling, "now you're starting to sound like a baby."

"I can't help it," she snapped and flopped her arms down on top of the quilt. Her fingertips idly played with a loose thread. "I hate being sick and I don't want you taking care of me."

"You've been taking care of me for years," he reminded her. "Consider this payback."

"A debt." She sighed. "Great. Perfect."

Now what had he done? "I'll be back in awhile."

"Apparently, I'll be here."

He left her then and went to call Maggie.

"This'll be good for him," Maggie said, smoothing the fresh linen case on the plumped pillow behind Kara's head. As she moved along the bed, tugging at the quilt, she walked through a slash of sunlight that gilded the lighter streaks in her dark hair. Smiling, she glanced at Kara. "Maybe what Cooper needs is to feel needed."

Kara wasn't so sure about that. In the years she'd known him, he'd made a point of never being indispensable to anyone. He never had relationships that lasted more than a few months. And until this summer, he hadn't even seen his family in years.

He wanted to be needed?

No, Kara didn't see that. She'd always thought that Cooper did everything he could to keep from being needed.

"He's making me crazy," Kara admitted as her stomach did another wild pitch and roll. She slapped one hand to her abdomen and swallowed hard, determined to get through the rest of the day without ending up on her knees in the bathroom. Inhaling deeply, determinedly, she said, "He hovers. He brings me tea I can't drink and crackers that make me want to heave. And then he just sits there and stares at me. And I look *hideous*."

Maggie chuckled then sat down in the chair beside the bed. "Apparently, Cooper doesn't agree. He's worried about you."

She'd like to think so, but reality kept rearing its ugly head to keep her from delving into fantasies best left alone. "It's not worry," she said on a sigh. "He said he's just paying me back for all the years I've been taking care of him."

Maggie shook her head, disbelieving. "Did he actually say that?"

"Yes. And," Kara added, "he feels bad for me because I got so sick right after—" Oops. No point in turning this little chat into a confessional.

But Maggie was too quick to be fooled. A pleased smile curved her mouth as she leaned back and lifted her feet to cross them on the edge of the bed. "Ah…so you finally managed to get him to *notice* you?"

Kara sighed again, this time in disgust. "Oh yeah. He noticed all right. Hard not to notice when the woman you're making love to suddenly has to make a break for the bathroom."

"Oh no." Maggie winced in sympathy. "Right in the middle?"

She shook her head. "Right after. In the middle of what was looking to be a truly great afterglow."

"Oh," Maggie said dreamily, "I do love the whole glow part."

"I wouldn't know," Kara said. "My glow was cut short."

"So, next time will be better."

"Next time?" Kara repeated on a disgusted groan. "There won't be a next time. He saw me sick as a dog. Held my head. Please. Any man who has to live through that is never going to look at that woman with passion again."

Maggie laughed.

Kara scowled at her. "So happy to give you your morning chuckle."

"Well come on, Kara." Still grinning, Maggie nudged her with her foot. "You think couples never see each other at their worst? Trust me. I'm sick every morning and every night, Sam's right there, pulling me in close and…" She cleared her throat. "Well, that's not the point."

"No you're right. It's not. That's completely different. You're *pregnant,*" Kara said, pointing an accusatory finger at her. "With Sam's child. Of course he's still sexually attracted to you. He *loves* you."

"Yeah," Maggie said with a contented sigh, "he really does. Are you so sure Cooper doesn't love you?"

Kara snorted and tugged a little harder at the loose string on the quilt, wrapping the thread around her index finger until the tip of it turned purple. "Love didn't have anything to do with it. At least not on his part. Trust me Maggie, I wish you were right. I wish he did love me. But he doesn't."

Another sigh wafted through the room. This one was deep, tormented, heartfelt. It came from nowhere. And everywhere.

Maggie dropped her feet to the floor and shot straight up in her chair, like someone had shoved a steel rod down the back of her tank top. "Was that…?"

Kara looked around the room and shrugged. "I'd introduce you but I don't know her name. So I'll just say, Maggie, meet our ghost. Ghost…Maggie."

He really had to get out of the frozen food section more often.

When left to his own devices, Cooper usually snatched up whatever edible looking frozen dinners he could find and called his shopping finished. Today, he'd gone up and down every aisle, the produce section and even the meat counter. Amazing really, what was out there.

He stacked a dozen grocery bags in the trunk of

his SUV, and slammed the lid shut. Then he looked around the quiet main street of Coleville and for the first time, really felt as though he'd come home.

Not much had changed and a part of him was grateful. Stupid really. He'd been avoiding this place for fifteen years because of the memories and now he was relieved to find it much as he'd left it.

A cool, sharp wind flew in off the ocean, dispelling some of the summer heat as Cooper walked toward the drugstore on the corner. Two kids rattled past him, surfing the sidewalks on skateboards whose wheels growled in their wake. An old woman lifted her suitcase-sized purse and shouted at them, but the kids didn't even slow down.

Cooper was still smiling to himself as he opened the door and heard the familiar clang and jangle of the old-fashioned bell over the door. God, when he and his cousins were kids, they'd been in and out of this store all summer. Candy bars, ice cold sodas and comic books were all he'd needed back then to make him happy.

And just for a second, Cooper wondered why life had to get so complicated.

He wandered through the aisles, nodding and smiling to the few people he passed. A refrigerated cabinet held a selection of flowers and before he could think twice about it, Cooper had the thing open and was reaching inside. Roses? He grabbed up a big bouquet of yellow roses, took a sniff, then stopped to think about it.

Did Kara like roses? He didn't know. And why the hell didn't he know? Five years they'd been together and he didn't know if she liked roses? He scowled down at the tight, colorful buds, then let his gaze sweep the interior of the case. There were a few mixed bouquets and a selection of carnations, daisies and some weird looking purple flower he couldn't identify.

"This shouldn't be so hard," he muttered, shifting his gaze from one bunch of flowers to the next as refrigerated air puffed out around him.

"Cooper Lonergan, shut that door! You think I'm paying to cool off the inside of the store?"

He jumped, startled and spun around to look down into Mrs. Russell's beady black eyes. The old woman had been a hundred and ten when Cooper was a boy, so he could only guess that she really had been an evil witch. Because she was still alive—and looking no friendlier than she had back in the old days.

"Sorry Mrs. Russell," he said and stepped back, still clutching the roses as he shut the glass doors. "Just trying to make up my mind."

She frowned at him and scuttled past toward the cash register behind the front counter. "Well, do your thinking with the door closed."

"Nice to see you, too," he muttered.

"Horrifying, isn't she?"

Cooper turned to face a tall pretty woman with

pale blond hair and deep blue eyes. She had a wire basket over one arm and a knowing smile on her face.

"Ah, yeah," he said, trying to figure out who she was. She looked at him as if he should know her, but for the life of him, he couldn't figure out how. "But then she always was."

The blond cast a quick glance to make sure Mrs. Russell was out of earshot before saying, "I think she's still holding a grudge against you and your cousins for the Fourth of July fiasco."

He smiled just thinking about it. Funny, he hadn't remembered that in years. He, Jake, Sam and Mac, eager for a little early celebration, had pooled their money and bought some illegal bottle rockets. They hadn't actually *planned* to launch one of them into the Russells' shed and burn it down.

Still smiling, he recalled, "And then Jeremiah made us spend the next three weeks building her a new shed."

"You got off easy," the blond said. "I was grounded for a month."

Cooper narrowed his gaze on her and just for a minute or two, the last fifteen years fell away and he saw her as she had been then. Tall and skinny, with wide blue eyes that were always locked on Mac. "Donna? Donna Barrett?"

"Hi, Cooper," she said, "it's good to see you again."

He swept her into a hard hug, then jumped back

as the bouquet of roses dripped water on her shoulder. "Sorry about that."

"No problem. I heard you and Sam had come home."

"Yeah. For the summer anyway. Jake's coming, too."

"All of you together again." Her voice went wistful, and her gaze dropped to the basket on her arm.

"Almost all of us," he said, knowing that Donna's thoughts were centered on Mac. And why wouldn't they be? Donna and Mac had lived in each other's pockets that last summer.

She'd become an unofficial part of their little group not just because the rest of them liked her, but because if they hadn't included her they wouldn't have seen much of Mac. In fact, the day Mac died, was only one of a handful of days Donna hadn't been with them. If she had been, maybe things would have been different. Maybe they wouldn't have waited so long to jump in after him. Maybe...

Silence stretched out between them as taut as an overextended rubber band as both of them drifted through the past, facing their regrets. Finally, he spoke up again, scrambling for something to say. "I heard you moved out of Coleville right after—"

Great. Perfect. Nice job, Cooper. Think of something else to say and go right back to that summer. But Donna played along.

"Yeah. I went to live with my aunt. In Colorado. Stayed there and went to school and now, well…" she shrugged and swept her hair back from her face. "It was time to come home." She waved one hand at the roses, now dripping water all over the linoleum. "So, hot date?"

He laughed uneasily. "No. Just trying to find flowers to bring to a…friend." *Friend?* Weak word. But what other word would do? *Lover?* Did one night together make them lovers? Not if Kara was to be believed. She was already trying to find a way to wipe that incident from her memory and his.

"She'll love them."

"You think?" He stared at them as if expecting them to change color or something. "All women like roses, right?"

One blond eyebrow lifted. "We're not interchangeable, Cooper."

"I know, I just meant—hell." He didn't know what he meant. Never before had he been so at a loss as to how to treat a woman. But Kara was different. She had a place in his life. She was…special.

Right. So special he didn't even know if she liked roses or not.

Well, he could solve that problem at least, he told himself and opened the refrigerated door again. Grabbing up all of the other bouquets, he figured that the one sure way to get Kara's favorite flower, would be to buy all of them.

"Making a statement?" she asked, laughing.

"No," he said, resisting the idea—even the vague hint of the idea—that he might be trying to win someone's heart. That wasn't what this was about. This was about being nice to someone he…cared for. About wanting to make Kara feel a little less crappy. "Just buying too many flowers," he said firmly.

From outside, a car horn blasted three or four times in short, impatient bursts. Donna threw a quick look over her shoulder at the wide windows overlooking the street. Then she turned back to Cooper, and said, "It was good to see you, but I've really got to run."

"Everything okay, Donna?" She looked…nervous all of a sudden.

"Fine." She hurried to Mrs. Russell at the cash register. "I hope your friend likes her flowers."

"Yeah, me, too." Thoughtfully, he watched her leave the store, and hurry to a pickup truck. There was someone in the passenger seat, but thanks to the sun's glare on the windshield, Cooper couldn't make out who it might be.

Then shaking his head, he told himself to forget about Donna Barrett. Whatever she had going on in her life now, he wished her well. But he had a sick woman at home and he didn't want to keep her waiting.

"Six bouquets?" Kara asked, astonished as Cooper carried in the last bunch of purple irises and set them across from her on top of the dresser.

He shrugged, shoved both hands into the pockets of his black slacks and said, "I didn't know—" he caught himself and started again. "They were all nice."

Kara smiled in spite of the disappointment she felt. Five years of knowing him, working with him every day and he didn't even know this one small thing about her. "You didn't know what kind of flowers I like."

He frowned and pulled one hand free long enough to stab his fingers through his hair. In a disgusted grumble he admitted, "No, I didn't. I did know you like flowers, though."

"Uh-huh." Thank God, her stomach had stopped its rumbling and spinning. Otherwise the combined scents of the fresh flowers would have had her running for the bathroom again. Now, it was just giving her a headache.

But he looked so pleased with himself, it was hard to burst his bubble.

"It was sweet of you to think of it," she said finally, trying to let go of her old dreams and see him as he really was. Did it matter that he didn't know what kind of flower she liked? Wasn't it more important that he'd thought of the act at all? "Thank you, Cooper."

He beamed at her, then reached for the shopping bag he'd dumped unceremoniously at the bedroom door. "I brought these, too. And stared Mrs. Russell, the old bat, right in the eye while I paid for them."

"What are you talking ab—" she broke off and smiled as he pulled five magazines from the bag and laid them on the bed beside her. Magazines about fashion and hair and gossip, he'd picked up exactly what he thought a woman would read. "Thanks, they're great."

"So how about soup?" he asked in a coaxing voice, "I bought chicken and stars."

"You don't have to fix my dinner, Cooper. Why don't you just go out and get something for yourself."

"Get something?" He managed to look both proud and insulted. "I bought steaks at the market and I'll be cooking my own dinner."

"Really?"

"I'm not completely useless, Kara."

"I never said *useless*," she corrected. "I believe the word I used was *hopeless*."

"Is that right?" He moved around the edge of her bed and straightened the quilt laying over her. "Well, I not only grocery shopped, but I did a couple of loads of laundry—did you know you can overfill a washing machine?"

"How big a mess was it?"

"The floors are clean."

"Cooper…"

"And, I even did some ironing."

She stared up at him, amazed and just a little sad. "You ironed?"

"Not for long," he admitted with a shrug. "The

plastic cover on that ironing board in the pantry? Why would they want you to put something hot on a covering that can melt?"

"You didn't."

"I'll buy a new iron," he said, brushing aside his little domestic disaster.

"Cooper," Kara said softly, "why are you doing all this? Really."

He stopped, looked down at her and gave her one of those smiles that could turn her inside out in a heartbeat. "Because I want to. Now, about that soup?"

Kara nodded, but didn't speak because she was just a little bit afraid that her voice might break if she tried. She watched him leave the room and when he was gone, she shifted her gaze to stare up at the late afternoon sunlight playing across the beamed ceiling. The scent of fresh flowers surrounded her and from somewhere in the room came the softest of sighs.

Not only was Cooper surviving without her…he appeared to be thriving.

Eight

"How're you holding up?" Sam set his medical bag onto the kitchen table and gave his cousin a stern look.

Morning sunlight shone in the room and Cooper squinted against the brightness while he cupped a full coffee mug between his palms. Lifting it for a sip, he shuddered at the taste and made a mental note to ask Kara *again* how to brew a decent pot of caffeine.

"I'm great," he said tightly, then dropped into a kitchen chair before he fell down. He felt as though he hadn't slept in weeks. "Now why don't you tell me about the patient you actually came here to see."

Sam shook his head and wandered over to the coffeepot. Grabbing down a cup from the cabinet, he filled the mug, took a sip and grimaced. "How can anybody screw up coffee this badly?"

"It's a gift," Cooper said, bracing one elbow on the table. "How's Kara?"

"She's fine. Probably better than you," Sam said, leaning back against the counter. "Did I mention that you look like hell?"

"Thanks." He took another gulp of coffee—not because he was getting used to the taste, but because the caffeine was the only thing keeping him awake. "She's okay? Really?"

"Yeah. I told you before, it was just the flu." Sam checked his wristwatch, took another sip of coffee, then choked it down before setting the almost full cup aside. "She's tired and weak, but she'll get better. Give her a couple more days to rest up. Keep her on light foods, a bland diet."

"Bland I can manage," Cooper muttered.

"Maggie would be happy to come over and help you out."

"No," he said. "I can take care of Kara. I want to."

"Hmm." Sam walked to the table, sat down opposite Cooper and stared at him thoughtfully.

"What?"

"Nothing. This is just interesting. I've never known you to have a domestic side."

"Cute." Cooper leaned back in his chair and said with a choked laugh, "Hell, Sam. I had no idea there was so much to do every day. I don't know how the hell Kara does it all. She never gets shook. Always has things organized. And never so much as has a nervous breakdown. Seriously, I haven't been paying her nearly enough money."

"I'm sure she'll be glad to hear that," Sam mused.

Cooper didn't even hear him. "I've spent so much time on the phone, dealing with my editor and agent and publicist, not to mention trying to get Kara to eat some soup and do laundry without flooding the place, I haven't written a word in two days."

"Or slept?"

Wryly, Cooper smiled. "Yeah. I've been sitting in a chair beside Kara in case she wakes up and needs something."

"Uh-huh." Sam shifted in his seat, threw one arm across the back of the chair and smiled to himself.

"Whatever you're thinking," Cooper told him, "forget it."

Sam drummed the fingers of his left hand against the tabletop. "Okay. If you don't want to talk about Kara, then why don't we talk about you?"

Cooper groaned inwardly. He was in no shape to be analyzed and Sam definitely had that "look" in his eyes. The look that said, *I know what your problem is and I have the solution.*

"Sam," Cooper said softly, "take pity on an exhausted man. Give me a break."

"You've been here for a few weeks now," Sam

said softly, completely ignoring Cooper's plea. "As far as I know, you still haven't been out to the lake."

Cooper's grip tightened on the handle of the mug until his knuckles went white. Fatigue pulled at him, but he stiffened despite the slump in his shoulders. "No, I haven't. Don't plan to, either."

Sam looked disappointed, somehow. "Damn it, Cooper. You can't keep hiding from that day."

Something squirmed in his guts and Cooper fought the urge to shift uncomfortably in his chair. "It's worked for me this long."

"You're here," Sam said quietly. "You came all the way to Coleville. Why not take it the rest of the way?"

"I came for Jeremiah's sake. I'm not here to relive the past." Deliberately, Cooper released his grip on the coffee mug and sat back in his chair. "I was in town the other day," he said, noting that Sam looked irritated by the change of subject. "I saw Donna."

"Barrett?" Surprised, Sam stared at him for a long minute. "I didn't know she was in town."

"Apparently, she's moved back."

"How's she look?"

"Good. But that's not my point," Cooper said, pushing his coffee cup away from him and leaning both forearms on the table as if he couldn't quite hold himself up straight in the chair without support. "I saw her and instantly, my mind went back to that summer. I could feel the sun. Smell the ocean." He sighed.

"Hell, Sam, I could have sworn I actually heard Mac laugh. It was all so close. Just by seeing Donna."

"Cooper…"

He looked into Sam's eyes and shook his head solemnly. "No. I buried the past, Sam. And I'm going to keep it buried."

Sam watched him for a few long seconds then sighed. "It's not buried, Cooper. It's with you every damn day. And until you face it—face *Mac*—you'll never really be free of it."

After Sam had gone, Cooper sat alone in the sun drenched kitchen and felt cold pressing in on him. Whether it was the ghost in the house or the ghosts in his own mind, Cooper acknowledged the truth. He didn't deserve to be free of the past.

He deserved to be haunted.

Kara pushed herself weakly into a sitting position against the pillows propped up on the headboard of the bed. She was finally starting to feel alive again. Barely. At least her stomach had stopped churning every few minutes. But she also felt like a slug. She hadn't even been able to work up the energy to crawl into the shower.

"How you feeling?"

She snapped a look at the doorway. Cooper stood there, leaning one shoulder against the doorjamb. Hands in his pockets, one foot crossed over the other, he looked tired. And impossibly good.

The last couple of days had been so hard. Not only feeling like death, but being so close to him. Having Cooper sit up at her side all through the night and knowing that he wasn't doing it because he loved her, but because he felt he owed her.

He pushed away from the door and walked toward her slowly. Kara grabbed at the quilt covering her and pulled it up higher, covering her chest, wanting to pull it up over her head. She knew what she must look like. She'd caught a brief glimpse of herself in the bathroom mirror earlier and had yelped in fright.

"Kara?" He waved one hand back and forth in front of her face. "You're zoning again."

"I didn't zone. I'm in a coma."

"Pretty chatty for a coma."

"Was there a reason for this visit?"

Twin black eyebrows lifted. "Should you still be this crabby now that you're getting better?"

"Cooper…"

"Relax. I only came to see if you felt well enough to try a shower."

She blinked at him, trying to dislodge a sudden, extremely clear image of the two of them, naked, wrapped together under a stream of hot water. His hands, slick with soap, sliding over her body, dipping between her legs, stroking, while his mouth…

"Kara?"

She came up out of the fantasy and gave herself a mental kick. Oh, sleeping with him had been a *big* mistake. Now she knew what she'd be missing for the rest of her life. And in her heart, she knew damn well there wasn't another man alive who would ever compare to Cooper Lonergan.

But the simple truth was, he wasn't hers and never would be. Might as well get used to that fact.

"I heard you," she said and threw the quilt back. Cool air hit her bare legs and she shivered. "And the answer is yes. I'm definitely willing to give it a try."

"Hey, not so fast," he cautioned, moving in to grab one of her arms as she jumped to her feet.

"I'm fine," she said, "I can do this myself—" She swayed unsteadily and leaned into his hard, muscled chest. The room did a nasty little tilt and she closed her eyes to steady herself. "Okay," she acknowledged a few seconds later, "maybe I could use a little help."

"You've been flat on your back for nearly three days, Kara." He wrapped one arm around her waist and Kara could have sworn she felt five separate stabs of heat from each of his fingers.

"You haven't had any food in your system," he reminded her. "So take it easy until you get your strength back, okay?"

His voice was tight, and she was pretty sure she heard his heart pounding out a frantic rhythm. Kara wasn't sure if it was worry or desire causing the jump in his blood pressure but decided to go with worry. Since that thought was less likely to break her heart.

Patting his chest, she straightened up, backing out of his embrace and then took a single step, wishing her legs didn't feel quite so wet-noodley. Her head spun crazily and her vision went a little fluffy at the edges.

"Whoa. Interesting sensation," she whispered just before Cooper scooped her up into his arms.

"Okay, we'll do this another way." He cradled her close and Kara indulged herself. Laying her head on his shoulder, she inhaled the scent of him—soap, shampoo and the spicy zing of his aftershave.

Her stomach wobbled, but it had nothing to do with the flu. It was simply the effect Cooper had on her. Only now, it was worse than ever before because she knew what it was to have him inside her. To feel his mouth on her skin, his hands on her body. She knew the shattering sensation of climaxes rippling through her system and the brush of his breath against her neck.

And oh, she wanted it all again.

Even knowing that it was going nowhere.

That he would never love her.

She wanted him so much, everything in her yearned.

"You okay?" he whispered, his breath dusting the top of her head.

"Yeah," she insisted firmly. "Just a little light-headed is all."

He left the bedroom, walked down the hall and stepped into the bathroom. The walls were a cool green and the old tile floor was laid in a pattern of green-and-white checks.

"You want me to help you?" he asked as he set her down onto her feet.

"No," she said, though her mind was screaming *yes!* No point in making this even harder on herself. Her shower fantasy burst once again into full bloom in her brain, and the images it produced left her nearly breathless with a hunger that shook her right down to her bones. But she steeled herself against it, and met his gaze squarely. "I'll be fine."

He didn't look as if he believed her. But still, he backed up toward the door. "I'll be close if you need me. I'm gonna change the sheets on the bed."

Kara blinked. "You are?"

Scowling, Cooper said, "You know, I wish you'd quit looking at me like that."

"Like what?"

"Like I'm performing a miracle or something whenever I do something around here. I *am* capable of a few things."

She smiled at his insulted tone and tried to smooth his ruffled feelings. "Of course you are, it's just—"

"I know." He held up one hand to stop the rest of her explanation and gave her a half smile. "I've never done it before. But then, never really had to, did I?"

"No," she mused, thinking about how she was usually the one taking care of him. She'd worked so hard for so long to make herself indispensable to him, it had never occurred to her that maybe she'd done too much. "I guess not."

He nodded and stuffed both hands into his jeans pockets. "Oh yeah, you didn't have another nightgown that I could find, so I put one of my T-shirts in there for you to wear while your nightgown gets washed."

She glanced down and saw his neatly folded white T-shirt. He'd even thought of this. She'd been in her nightgown for nearly three days now and she could hardly wait to get out of it. "More laundry?"

He shrugged and smiled. "Think I'm getting the hang of it."

"Thanks," she said, "for thinking of it."

"No problem," he said, backing the rest of the way out of the bathroom. "And if you get dizzy again, while you're taking a shower, for God's sake, sit down."

"I will."

He stopped. "Maybe I should just stay in the room with you, just in case…"

Oh, that's all she needed.

"Go away," she said, laying one hand on his chest and pushing him out of the room.

She closed the door and leaned back against it for a long minute or two, trying to keep from opening it again and inviting him inside. Then she heard his footsteps moving off down the hall and she sighed. In disappointment or relief…she wasn't sure.

Then shaking her head, she peeled off her nightgown and headed for the shower.

* * *

In the darkness, Cooper sat alongside the bed and watched Kara sleep. Moonlight spilled across the mattress illuminating her in a silvery light that made her already pale skin glow like fine porcelain. Her eyelashes were long and lay curved on her cheeks in a smudge of darkness that was vulnerable as well as tempting.

He sucked in a breath of air and blew it out again while leaning forward, forearms braced on his thighs. He couldn't seem to stop watching her and he wondered why he'd never noticed before just how beautiful she was. She sighed and shifted in her sleep, the quilt sliding down, baring her shoulder and the plain white T-shirt that covered her.

Damn, who would have thought a woman could look that good in a man's shirt? He could still see her, coming out of the bathroom. The hem of the T-shirt hit just beneath her bottom, baring her long, lean legs to his gaze. Her hair, freshly washed and dried, drifted around her shoulders in thick, tempting waves and her eyes, though still shadowed, looked clear for the first time in days.

His fingers itched to stroke her skin again as memory after memory rushed into his brain, crowding it with the images and sounds and scents of their lovemaking. Only a few nights ago, she'd opened herself to him and he'd discovered a depth and passion he hadn't expected.

His body stirred, tightening with a hunger that clawed at his insides until he wanted to howl with need. And he called himself all kinds of a bastard for wanting her when she was so clearly exhausted.

He leaned back in his chair and then jolted upright when an unearthly howl erupted from the bowels of the house. Jumping to his feet, he stared around the room, but it did no good. The wailing came from nowhere and everywhere. It seemed to seep from the walls as if even the house itself were keening in misery.

"Damn it," he muttered, swallowing past the knot lodged in his throat. It had been a couple of days since the ghost had made itself known. Cooper had almost begun to think that it had decided to leave them the hell alone.

Now though, it was back and louder than ever.

Another heartrending wail sobbed around him, sending a chill washing through him. Outside, a wind kicked up out of nowhere, rattling the window panes. Bits of dirt and pebbles were thrown high, pinging off the glass like eager fingers tapping, tapping, demanding entry.

The temperature in the room dropped suddenly and as the sobbing continued, cold gathered. Cooper moved closer to the bed, standing with his back to Kara, so that he stood as a sentry, between her and the growing cold.

Even as he did it though, he fought down a sharp laugh. What the hell could he do to a ghost? What he should do was grab up Kara and get her some-where…else. But he'd be damned if he was going to be chased out of his own house by the psychic energies of one long-dead woman and her erstwhile lover.

"Get out," he muttered thickly, and the sobbing throbbed in the air.

"Cooper?"

He spun around to find Kara sitting up in bed, pushing her hair back out of her eyes and looking around the empty room.

"She just started up," he muttered, glaring at the shadows as if trying to intimidate the spirit into silence.

Another howl was his answer. The sound rippled along his skin, and lifted the hair at the back of his neck.

"She's lonely," Kara whispered.

"She's *nuts,*" Cooper countered.

A disembodied moan whined around them.

Kara reached for his hand and pulled him down onto the bed beside her. He sat down, back braced against the headboard and pulled her in close, if only to keep her warm in the bone numbing cold.

"She shouldn't have waited for him for so long," Kara said, her voice almost lost in the weeping.

Cooper shook his head, amazed that they were sitting in the dark, discussing the feelings of a woman long dead. "Hell, she'd waited two years. Maybe she should have waited a little longer. He *did* show up finally."

"Too late," Kara reminded.

"It didn't have to be too late," he said, raising his voice to be sure even the ghost heard him. "If she hadn't curled up and died, they could have been together. He's outside the house right now and she *still* won't let him in."

Kara looked up at his profile in the darkness and tried not to make too much of his words. The problem was, she wanted to believe that he was trying, subconsciously even, to tell her to not give up on him.

But if she started believing things like that, she'd only be setting herself up for the same kind of misery that haunted the woman trapped in this house.

Better if she did what that woman had not done.

Give up on the dream and move on.

Nine

Kara reluctantly woke up from the most erotic dream she'd ever experienced, to silent darkness. Apparently the ghost had given up for the night.

So what then had woken her?

An instant later, she knew. In her dream, Cooper's hands had moved over her body with smooth deliberation, caressing, stroking, driving her toward a climax she knew would be soul shattering.

Now that she was awake, she realized the dream was real. Cooper lay right behind her, spooned up along her back. At some point during the night, he'd undressed, because the heat from his naked body rushed into hers and she felt the hard, solid length of his erection pressing against her behind.

Yet even that delicious sensation was trumped by the feel of one of his hands cupped between her thighs. Damp heat pooled in her center and her breath staggered past a knot of need lodged in her throat.

Instinctively, she parted her thighs for him, silently asking that he touch her more surely, more deeply. Closing her eyes, she shifted against his hand, delighting in the frisson of sensations that swept through her in a rush. His fingers moved on her, dipping into her warmth, sliding over the tender, sensitive flesh.

She sighed and his name came out on a groan. "Cooper..."

"Right here," he whispered, bending his head to the curve of her neck, nibbling, licking.

"Yeah," she said breathlessly, "I got that..."

He smiled against her skin, then nibbled a little harder. "Sorry I woke you."

"No," she said, "you're not." Smiling, she gulped in another breath as his fingers continued their gentle invasion.

"Okay," he admitted, "I'm not."

She rolled over onto her back and stared up into his dark eyes. While she watched him, he dipped one finger and then two inside her and she swallowed hard, loving the feeling of him touching her so deeply. When her nerve endings stopped frying, she managed to ask, "What're you doing, Cooper?"

In the pale wash of moonlight, she saw one dark eyebrow lift. "I would have thought that was obvious."

She sucked in a breath as he shifted his grip on her and stroked a nearly electrically charged nubbin of flesh.

"Yes," Kara choked out a laugh that was just the tiniest bit hysterical. "I guess I meant, *why?* Why are you…we…" she lifted her hips, arching into his hand, "…oh, boy, that really feels so good."

"Yeah," he murmured, dusting a hard, brief kiss on her mouth. "It really does."

Fighting to maintain, to hold onto some semblance of her dignity—which Kara was beginning to think was way overrated—she shook her head on the pillow and demanded, "Is this some sort of sympathy thing?"

"What?"

"You know," she said, pausing as his fingers once again plumbed her depths, pressing, stroking. "Wow, you're good at this," she said even while her brain shrieked at her to think.

"It's a gift," he said, kissing her again, drawing the tip of his tongue along her bottom lip.

Deliberately, she focused her splintering concentration even while her hips rocked, setting a rhythm she ached to give herself up to. "But Cooper—I don't want a pity orgasm."

"*Huh?*"

"I've been sick and you want to make me feel better and—"

"You're crazy," he said, his voice filled with wonder. "I never knew that about you."

"I'm not crazy," she countered, trying not to notice that he was rubbing that sensitive spot again, "I'm just not interested in a 'poor little Kara, let's give her a ride' night."

His hand on her stilled, his palm pressed tight against her heat. "What're you talking about?"

"Come on, Cooper," she said, fighting to keep from begging him to rub her again. To stroke her inside and out. To push her over the edge into those fireworks she remembered so well from their one night together.

Her hips moved again, seemingly of their own accord. Apparently her body was smarter than she was. It didn't care why he was offering up an orgasm, it just wanted one.

But Kara ignored the tantalizing rush of sensation. Fought to keep her mind focused on what she knew to be true. To keep her from allowing him to do something that would mean nothing to him and, therefore, little to her.

Shaking her head, she met his gaze and said it, plain and simple. "You saw me sick as a dog, Cooper. You can't be feeling attracted to me after that disgusting display, so this has got to be some warped sense of a good deed—or—I don't know."

"You *are* nuts," Cooper said, spearing his fingers

up into her damp heat again, groaning as her head tipped back into the pillows.

"Cooper…"

"Look at me," he ordered thickly, his voice a raw scrape of sound. When her gaze was locked with his, he said, "I've been wanting you for days. I even wanted you when you were sick. Hell, there you were, bent over a toilet and all I could think about was what a cute behind you've got. How twisted is *that?*"

Kara ground her hips against his hand. "Really?"

"Really." He stroked her inner folds, driving her to the brink of desperation, only to pull her back from the edge and taunt her toward it again. "And," he said, dipping his head to claim a kiss, "I know you're still exhausted. Haven't had a good night's sleep in three nights, and am I letting you rest? Nope. I'm waking you up and hoping to hell you want me as badly as I want you."

"Really?"

"Will you stop saying that?" He dropped another kiss on her mouth, ran the tip of his tongue across her lips.

"Right," she murmured, expelling a long breath on a deep groan.

"So? Are you with me here, Kara? Or should I let you go to sleep?"

"Who needs sleep?" she asked breathlessly, opening her thighs for him, reaching up to wrap her arms around his neck.

"I was so hoping you'd say that," he admitted, dipping his head to nibble at the line of her throat as she tilted her head back, deeper into the pillow.

Kara finally stopped thinking.

Stopped questioning his motives.

And gave herself up to the pure pleasure swamping her.

Again and again, his clever fingers worked on her body even as he slid farther down and used his free hand to push up the hem of the T-shirt she wore. When her breasts were bared to the moonlight, he took first one hardened nipple into his mouth and then the other. Over and over, he suckled her, drawing on her skin as if trying to sip her being into his.

Dizzying sensations jolted through her and Kara could hardly keep up with them all. It felt as though her entire body were on fire and she encouraged the flames. She wanted them hotter, brighter. She wanted to be engulfed in the heat that was Cooper.

Shifting over her, he moved down her body, trailing damp kisses along her flesh. She grabbed at him, trying to pull him up for a kiss. To feel his mouth on her own. But he neatly avoided her grasping hands and settled himself between her thighs with an anticipatory sigh.

Opening her eyes, she looked at him and her breath caught. In the wash of moonlight pearling through the windows, his dark eyes gleamed with temptation and his tanned, hard body shone like marble.

"Cooper…"

"Shut up, Kara," he whispered with a smile. Then he lifted her hips off the mattress, slung her legs over his shoulders and covered her heat with his mouth.

She shrieked.

Kara heard her own voice ricocheting off the walls, but she couldn't care. Couldn't do anything but feel.

His lips, teeth and tongue took her higher, faster than anything ever had before. She fisted her hands in the sheet beneath her, trying desperately to keep that one little grip on sanity as her brain fractured in a wash of fiery sparks.

He suckled her here, too. And while his mouth did amazing things to her, he managed to slide one finger into her depths, doing to her from the inside what his mouth was accomplishing on the outside.

"Too much," she whispered brokenly. "All too much. I can't. Cooper, I can't—"

He chuckled and her eyes went wide even as her body stiffened at the approaching climax. She felt it build at a fever pitch and wondered absently if she'd survive. Then she knew she didn't care. She would risk anything to feel this. To have this man in this moment.

That one sensitive bud at her core felt as though it were electrified and when Cooper lapped at it with the tip of his tongue, Kara shrieked again. His big hands cupped her behind and held her steady as she shouted his name and rocked her hips wildly in his grasp.

Releasing her death grip on the sheets, she reached for him and as a raw, charging fury raced through her body, she held his head to her and watched him as he took her over the edge.

Her body still trembling, still humming with the incredible power of her orgasm, Cooper knew he couldn't wait another moment. He had to be inside her. Had to feel her body surrounding his, feel the internal tremors as her muscles fisted around his length, squeezing him dry.

Heart pounding erratically, Cooper laid her down onto the mattress and stretched out a hand to the bedside table. Blindly, desperately, he yanked the drawer open and didn't even blink when it fell free of the table and landed upside down on the floor. He couldn't care about anything. Not now. Not after tasting her surrender. Not after holding her while a storm crested within her.

Not after experiencing Kara's climax with a force stronger than anything he'd ever known.

His only thought now was to feel it again. To be inside her when it came, to push himself so high and so deep within her body that the climax they would share would be incredible.

"Cooper…?"

"Just a minute." He scrambled off the edge of the bed, tossed the drawer to one side and grabbed up one of the foil packets that had fallen out. Quickly, he unwrapped it, sheathed himself and was back on the bed. His only regret was that he had to wear the damn condom in the first place. He wanted, more than anything, to feel her slick warmth on his skin. To feel the matchstick heat of sensation that could only come from two bodies, sliding together, unprotected from each other.

But he was too smart and too concerned for Kara to take that kind of chance.

Her arms opened to him as he rejoined her on the bed and he kissed her, taking her mouth while the taste of her body was still with him. His tongue swept inside her mouth, exploring, stroking, silently demanding.

And she gave as good as she got.

Their tongues met in an erotic dance, twining together, twisting, caressing until neither of them could draw a breath without a struggle. Her hands dropped from his back and tugged at the fabric of the shirt she still wore.

Groaning, Cooper eased back up and in one quick movement, had the shirt up and over her head and tossed into a heap on the floor.

"Better," she said, lifting her head from the pillow to claim his mouth again. She nibbled at his bottom lip and he felt an answering tug of need deep in the core of him.

"Gotta have you," he whispered, his lips moving over hers hungrily. Not enough, his brain shouted.

Not nearly enough. He wanted to taste every square inch of her body. Wanted her beneath him, over him, under him. He wanted her every way a man could want a woman and when they were finished, he wanted to do it all again.

And again.

"Yes," she said, moving to accommodate him as he shifted, kneeling between her legs.

He entered her with one swift thrust and she gasped at the invasion. Cooper paused, throwing his head back, staring blindly at the ceiling, concentrating solely on the lush feel of his body embedded in hers. But in an instant, need crowded within him and pushed him onward.

Bracing his hands at either side of her head, he rocked his hips against hers. She lifted her legs high, helping him to go deeper. He bent his head, tasted her nipples, rolling his tongue across their pebbly tips, one after the other. His hips pistoned, her sighs and moans echoed his. She tossed her head from side to side on the pillow. Licked her lips.

The sight of her tongue, darting across her parted lips enflamed him and Cooper bent to meet it. Then, staring into her eyes, he watched as flames erupted within her. Watched as passion glazed the surface of her deep green eyes and sparkled with the rush of completion.

He felt the clawing, clamoring ache within and fought to hold it off. He wanted it to last. Wanted this moment to never end. And in fact, the only reason he finally gave into his own release was because the only way to do this over again was to allow the climax to happen.

Her body erupted beneath his.

She called his name, her voice breaking.

And an instant later, Cooper groaned and followed her into the abyss.

Hours passed as they found each other again and again. Every muscle in Kara's body ached—and yet, she'd never felt more complete. More satisfied. Cooper had taken her in every way possible, she mused and in return, she'd taken him a couple of times, too.

And now, with the first streaks of dawn blurring the sky into a slow blossom of rich color, she lay in the circle of Cooper's arms and fell into an exhausted sleep…and a shared dream.

Cooper held her hand and Kara felt the warm strength of his fingers curled around hers. They stood in the parlor of the old Victorian—not as it was now, but as it had once been.

A piano stood in one corner of the room, sunlight streaming through the window to dance across the ivory keys. A paisley shawl was draped across the gleaming top of the piano and atop it, were a dozen or more framed, sepia-toned photographs. A black-

and-white cat was curled up in an overstuffed chair and at the wide front window, a woman stood.

Outlined in gilded light, she stared out the window at the road beyond, as if watching for someone. One hand to her mouth, she wrapped her other arm around her waist as if trying to comfort herself, when there was no comfort to be found.

Her quiet grief echoed in the room, and her tears looked like diamonds in the light. She kept watch, waiting for the lover who had promised to return. She walked from window to window, hope and fear keeping pace, her steps muffled on the carpets beneath her feet. Somewhere, a clock chimed out the hour and the woman's shoulders hunched with every soft gong.

Kara felt the woman's misery as if it were her own. Even the house itself seemed to throb with the pangs of the woman's agony. Time stood still, in this one little bubble of memory. For decades, the woman had been trapped—by her own pain and desperation and there didn't seem to be an end coming.

Kara looked up at Cooper and saw his eyes flash with pity just before a shutter dropped over them, locking her out.

She felt, as well as sensed, his withdrawal.

And in her sleep, Kara clung to him, afraid somehow that he would slip away from her and she would be left—like the crying woman—waiting for a love that would never be.

* * *

Cooper woke up first, half surprised to find that the dream was gone. Kara lay curled against him, her small hand on his chest. He covered it with one of his own, then reluctantly, let her go.

How had they shared that dream?

How had they been pulled into the ghost's pain and made to feel it with her? And how could he have forgotten, even for a second, the lessons he'd learned so long ago? Seeing the ghost as she'd once been, a young, beautiful woman who'd lost everything because she'd ventured to love, had reminded Cooper love meant pain.

Frowning, he eased out of the bed, stubbed his toe on the drawer, still laying on the floor, and bit back an angry oath. Staring down at the naked woman lying in his bed, something inside him turned over and he almost wished things could be different. But he knew, better than most, that they couldn't.

As if she felt his gaze on her, Kara woke up. Stirring languidly, she opened her eyes to meet his and gave him a tentative smile.

"Did we just—"

"Dream?" he asked, then nodded tightly, uneasy with the reborn feelings crashing around inside him. "Yeah, we must have."

"But how?"

"I don't know," he muttered and grabbed up his jeans off a nearby chair. He had to get out of that room. Had to keep from looking at Kara, or he'd slip. He'd forget about lessons learned and ghosts and old pains and lose himself in the arms of the woman who was, he suddenly realized, *way* too important to him. He couldn't let that happen, he told himself sternly, because he'd learned at a very early age, that to love only invited disaster.

"I'm going downstairs. Make some coffee."

"Cooper?"

He shook his head and chanced a quick look at her. Instantly, he realized his mistake. Love shone in her eyes and that terrified him. His heart went hard and cold in his chest and his throat tightened until he wasn't sure he'd be able to breathe.

He turned his back on her, because he couldn't look at her and not want her. Heading for the door, he grabbed hold of the brass knob, turned it and paused, door partially opened. "I'll bring you some coffee and maybe some eggs. I think you're well enough now to have some solid food."

"Okay," she said, her voice filled with questions he couldn't—wouldn't—answer. "But Cooper, we have to talk about—"

He shook his head and stepped out of the room. "Nothing to talk about, Kara. Dream's over. Time to wake up."

Ten

Two days later, things were still strained between Kara and Cooper. But actually, she thought, *strained* wasn't the right word. After all, he'd only reverted to normal.

He was back to being the closed off boss she knew so well. Distracted, preoccupied, Cooper spent most of his time locked away in his makeshift office. She heard the tapping of his fingers at the keyboard, but rarely saw him all day.

They still had dinner together in the kitchen, but there was no lighthearted chitchat. No teasing, no laughter. Nor was there any hint that their night of lovemaking was still haunting him as it was her.

The long nights passed slowly, Kara's only company, a ghost with whom she was beginning to think she had far too much in common.

"Serious thoughts?"

Kara looked up as Maggie approached and found a half-hearted smile to offer. "Very," she admitted and shifted her gaze to Cooper, standing on the opposite side of his grandfather's yard, talking to Jeremiah and Sam.

If he felt her gaze on him, he didn't let her know. He stood slightly apart from the other two men, as if keeping a careful distance even from his family. It broke Kara's heart, but she didn't have a clue how to fight it.

Maggie eased down onto the chair beside Kara's and stretched her long tanned legs out in front of her. She cupped her right hand over her still flat abdomen as if stroking the tiny child nestled within. "Oh, the shade feels great. I swear it's at least ten degrees cooler under this tree."

"Mmm-hmm." Kara was only half listening. Most of her focus was on Cooper. The heat rippled the air and made his image waver slightly as if he were already no more substantial than a dream. She squelched a sigh as she realized she couldn't even imagine her life without Cooper in it. But she would have to find a way to move on. Still, she couldn't look away from him. She'd made up her mind to finally leave him and now, all she had left were these unguarded times when she could look at him and store up as many mental snapshots as she could.

"You haven't told him that you love him, have you?"

Kara shot Maggie a glance, then shook her head. "No. There's no point. Trust me, it's not something he wants to hear."

"Maybe it's something he *needs* to hear, though," Maggie insisted, lifting her hair off her neck and then twisting it into a ponytail with a rubber band she tore off her wrist.

Kara would like to think so, but even knowing that Maggie meant well, the other woman didn't know Cooper as well as Kara did.

"Sam was the same way," Maggie continued, her voice softening as she shifted her gaze to where the three men stood talking. Sam and his grandfather were laughing at something and Cooper, aloof and alone, stood watching.

"What do you mean?" Kara asked, more to be polite than from real interest.

"I think what happened to Mac affected all of the cousins," Maggie said. "I know it's haunted Sam all these years, so I'm sure Cooper and Jake feel the same way. I mean, if you think about it, they were all only kids. And to have your cousin die like that…right in front of you…it must have been terrible for all of them."

Something cold slithered through Kara as she slowly swiveled her head to look at the woman sitting beside her.

Maggie caught her expression and read it correctly. She winced. "You didn't know any of this, did you?"

"No." God, it hurt to admit that. She'd been closer to Cooper than anyone else in his life for the last five years and he'd never said a word. Never let her in. Never gave a hint that there was something so horribly traumatic in his past. Here then was the reason for his withdrawal from life. For his refusal to let anyone past the walls he'd erected around his heart.

"I'm so sorry." Maggie reached out and laid her hand on Kara's. "I never would have said anything, but I assumed you knew."

"It's not your fault," Kara said, fighting the swell of regret and disappointment rising inside her.

"God, I'm an idiot."

"Tell me," Kara urged quietly.

"I don't know…" Maggie shook her head and looked as though she wished she were anywhere but there at the moment.

"Maggie, I have to know."

The other woman sighed, glanced at the men across the yard, then back to Kara. "Yes, I think you do."

While she talked, Kara's heart sank further. With every word she heard, the connection she'd felt to Cooper unraveled just a bit more. Like an old tapestry being torn apart, the fragile threads of their years together disintegrated. Tears filled her eyes, not only for the boy Cooper had once been and the tragedy of that long-ago summer day…but for the man he was now because of it. For chances lost, dreams crushed.

And Kara finally admitted the hard truth that she'd resisted for so long.

Cooper would never allow himself to love her.

Cooper watched Maggie and Kara, sitting in the shade of the old oak tree and wondered what the two women were talking about. Meanwhile, Jeremiah's and Sam's voices rattled in his ears, but he wasn't really listening. It was as if he was standing behind a glass wall. He could see them, but he was apart from them.

Hell, he'd been apart from everything for days now. Since he and Kara had shared that dream. Memories clouded his brain all the time. Whenever he closed his eyes, he saw Mac's face. He remembered that summer day fifteen years ago and how he'd vowed that he would never lose someone he loved again.

And the secret to that was to never love.

Caring too much was simply an invitation to pain.

That was why he'd cut himself off from his grandfather and his cousins. Losing Mac had hit him hard. As a kid, you think yourself immortal. Invulnerable. Learning differently had cut him nearly in two. Then his parents had died not long after that summer, reinforcing his decision to keep himself separate from any kind of closeness.

All he cared about now were his books. The imaginary people he interacted with on a daily basis. When one of them died, it didn't tear him up. Didn't rip out his heart and soul and leave it battered and bloody on the ground.

But then there was Kara. The feelings she pulled from him terrified him, plain and simple. A humbling thing for a man to admit, but there it was. He didn't want to care, damn it. And he resented like hell that she'd awakened something in him that had been long—and safely—dead.

And as much as he wanted to stalk across the yard, pull Kara from her chair and drag her home to bed…he knew that road could only end in pain.

So he stayed where he was. On the outside, looking in. Every night, he lay awake in his bed, afraid to sleep for fear of seeing Mac die again. And he couldn't lose himself in Kara because he knew he couldn't give her what she wanted and this way, though it cost him, he was able to spare Kara any more pain than was necessary.

He wasn't a complete idiot. He'd seen that happy little glow in her eyes the morning after they'd loved each other half to death. The shine of joy and pleasure and the dream of tomorrow had all been written there in her expression.

And he knew damn well that ignoring her now was hurting her. But how much better to be hurt now than devastated later? If he let her believe that there could be a future for them only to back away? No. It was better this way.

Not easier.

Better.

"What do you think?" Sam asked, snapping his fingers in front of Cooper's face.

"What?" He scowled at his cousin.

"Jeremiah and I were talking about re-doing Gran's old sewing room as a nursery," Sam said, and the tone of his voice said that this wasn't the first time he'd said it. "I asked what you thought."

"I think it's none of my business," Cooper pointed out and looked away from the slow head shake of disapproval his grandfather sent him.

"You're a big help," Sam muttered. "What the hell's wrong with you, anyway?"

"Not a damn thing," he said, disgusted that he'd let his own feelings be seen so easily. Starting for the house, he asked, "I'm going for a beer. You two want one?"

"Yeah," Sam said.

"Not for me." Jeremiah lifted his still half-full bottle in explanation.

"Fine." Cooper stalked across the grassy yard and headed for the house as a dying man in the desert aimed for the only oasis for miles. He just needed a little space. Some time alone. Some time to get away from everyone who was watching him in either hope or disappointment.

He couldn't give any of them what they wanted. Didn't they see that?

As he hit the front step, he paused to listen. The low growl of a motorcycle engine cut through the air and halted Jeremiah and Sam's conversation. The deep rumble of power rolled toward them, heralding the approach of a man who could only be Jake, the last Lonergan cousin.

Beer forgotten for the moment, Cooper stood stock-still and waited.

Sheba, the puppy who thought of herself as a Great Dane, set up a barking, howling discord to alert everyone just in case they hadn't heard the same noise she had. Then the little dog ran to Jeremiah and cowered behind his overall-clad legs as a huge motorcycle, chrome gleaming, prowled into the yard.

Sam and Jeremiah were there in seconds, leaving Cooper to study the situation from a safe distance. Jake turned off the engine and climbed off the bike, one hand extended to Sam. Jake's long black hair fell down the middle of his back in a ponytail. He wore a white T-shirt, black jeans and scuffed black boots that looked as though they'd walked to hell and back. A United States Marine Corps tattoo colored Jake's right bicep and two days' worth of beard shadowed his jaws. He yanked off wraparound sunglasses as he grinned at Sam.

"Good to see you, man."

"You, too. Nice bike."

"It rides," Jake said with a shrug, then turned to grin at his grandfather. "Jeremiah. You're looking a lot less dead than I expected."

"Good to have you home, boy," the older man said and swept his last remaining grandson into a fierce embrace.

Maggie and Kara were headed across the yard toward the commotion when Jake turned to look at Cooper. "There's the World Famous Author," he said, his tone putting the words in capital letters. "Read the last one. Scared the hell outta me."

Cooper smiled and walked the few steps toward his cousin. "Thanks." Then he held out one hand and as his cousin grabbed it, he said, "It's good to see you, Jake."

The Lonergan boys were together again.

Was he the only one feeling Mac's absence so intensely?

"Same here." Then Jake's dark eyes lit up as he spotted the women. "And who are the gorgeous ladies?" he asked, a well-practiced smile on his face.

"Cut your engines," Sam said, laughing, as he grabbed Maggie into a tight hug. "This one's mine."

"Well then," Jake continued, not even missing a beat as he stepped up to Kara and gave her a wink, "That leaves you and me. Unless…" he turned to look at Cooper, a question in his eyes.

Everything in Cooper yearned to knock Jake back a step. To drape one arm around Kara's shoulder and announce that she was *his*. But he couldn't do it. Not to her. Not to himself.

Instead, he forced himself to shrug and said, "Jake, this is Kara. My…" Did she take a breath and hold it? Waiting to see how he would introduce her? Could anyone else in the yard feel that near tangible tension that suddenly sprang up between them? Or was he imagining more than was there? "…assistant," he finally finished and then he watched as the expectant light in Kara's eyes flickered out.

Coolly then, as if she and Cooper hadn't just shared a knowing look, she gave her hand to Jake and smiled up at him. "It's a pleasure to meet you. Cooper's told me nothing about you."

Jake took her hand and threaded it through the curve of his arm. "I can take care of that," he said and gave her another wink. "As soon as I get some food in me. It's been a long ride."

"Hell, yes," Jeremiah shouted enthusiastically, as if trying to fill the sudden, yawning void that had opened up in front of them. "We've got steaks in the fridge. Sam, fire up the grill and Maggie, how about you and Kara do up some potatoes?"

"No problem," Maggie retorted and slipped out of Sam's grasp with a quick kiss. Then as she passed Kara, she asked, "Mind helping me out?"

"Not a bit," Kara said smoothly and stepped away from Jake.

As she walked past Cooper, he caught her scent

on the air and inhaled deeply. He whispered her name, not sure what it was he wanted to say—or even if there was anything he could say that would make things less awkward between them. All he knew was, he had to try.

But if she heard, she paid no attention. She deliberately passed him by, as if he weren't even there.

And wasn't that what he wanted?

Kara wanted to cry, but damn it, she wasn't going to.

She'd done this to herself and she knew it. That knowledge though, didn't make this any easier to take. She'd set herself up. Let herself dream idle fantasies about Cooper and how it could be for them.

But the simple truth was, Cooper didn't want her. A couple of nights between the sheets—no matter how fabulous they'd been—didn't make a relationship. And she wasn't willing to settle for anything less.

Now, after talking to Maggie and spending the evening watching Cooper avoid being drawn into stories about the old days, she knew there was no more hope. He hadn't only pulled away from her, he'd also shut himself away from his own family.

"What're you doing?"

Cooper's voice came from behind her and though it startled her, she didn't turn around to look at him. Instead, she picked up her yellow blouse from the bed, folded it neatly and tucked it into the open suitcase in front of her.

"I'm leaving."

"What?" He stepped into the room, walked to her side and stared from the suitcase to her. "*Now?*"

"Yes, now." She swallowed hard, inhaled sharply and blinked furiously, to keep any tears at bay. She wouldn't cry in front of him. Wouldn't let him see that her heart was breaking.

"Were you even going to tell me?"

She glanced at him. His mouth was grim, lips pressed tightly together. "Of course I was, Cooper." She reached past him for the denim skirt she'd brought with her and never wore. Folding it neatly, she laid it into the case. "Besides, I already gave you my two weeks' notice, remember?"

"Yeah, but—" He stalked to the end of the bed, then came right back again. "I didn't think you meant it."

"Now you know."

"Damn it, Kara…" He shoved both hands through his hair then pushed them into the back pockets of his jeans. "What's this really about? I know you like your job, so—"

"Cooper," she said on a sigh, "you know darn well what it's about."

"It's about us, then." He nodded stiffly, pulled one hand free of his pocket to scrape it across his face. "It's about the other night and that dream and the damn ghost and—"

Kara shook her head, grabbed up the last of her blouses and tucked it away. "This has *nothing* to do with the ghost and *everything* to do with us. Well, me, really."

"Kara," he said softly, voice filled with regret, "I just can't give you what you want."

Oh, she knew that. Felt it. Deep in her bones. And she wanted to weep with the knowledge. But that wouldn't do the slightest bit of good.

"Cooper," she said softly, lifting her gaze to his. "Why didn't you tell me about Mac?"

He backed up a step and stared at her for a long minute. "Where did you—oh. Maggie."

"Yes, Maggie."

"She shouldn't have told you."

"You're right," Kara said quietly. "You should have."

He shook his head firmly, shutting out her statement and the remote chance that she might be right. "It was a long time ago."

"No," she argued. "For you, it was yesterday."

He sucked in a gulp of air. "I don't want to talk about this."

"I know that, too," she said and walked to him. Laying both hands on his arms, she felt the tension in his muscles. Felt the rigid self-control he was drawing on and her heart hurt for him. "It wasn't your fault, Cooper. It wasn't anyone's fault."

He blew out a breath. "You don't know."

"Maggie told me what happened."

"She wasn't there. Neither were you."

"You were a kid, Cooper."

He stepped out from under her touch and the shutters were back in his eyes, closing her out. "So was Mac."

The tips of her fingers still hummed with warmth as if she could still feel his skin beneath hers. But there was no point in pretending any longer. There would be no future with a man who couldn't see past his own pain to the promise of something beautiful.

Still, she had to try to help him. One last time. "There was nothing you could have done. Maggie told me that Mac broke his neck when he jumped in."

Cooper actually flinched at her words as if they were a physical blow. He swallowed hard and jerked a nod. "He did. He was trying to beat Jake and his jump did it. But he had to stay underwater longer, too."

Kara tried reaching out for him, but he shook his head firmly. "You wanted to know, well here's what Maggie couldn't tell you," he said tightly. "Sam wanted to go in after Mac. He was worried. Jake was pissed off about losing, but I was *glad.*" He slapped one hand against his chest as a choked off, harsh laugh shot from his throat. "I was *happy* that Mac was staying under so long. Glad Jake was finally getting beaten. *I* talked Sam into waiting longer. If I hadn't…" his voice trailed off. "We'll never know

now. We might have saved him. If I'd just gone along with Sam and jumped in after Mac, he might still be alive. So don't tell me you understand. You couldn't."

"No," Kara said softly, empathetic pain rippling through her in response to the torment she read in Cooper's eyes—heard in his voice. "I can't know what you feel. What your regrets are. But I do know that Mac wouldn't want you torturing yourself forever over something that can't be changed."

His mouth worked as if he were grinding his teeth. "I loved him like a brother. And he died while we all stood there like morons."

"You didn't know."

"We *should* have known," Cooper countered quickly. "Should have felt it. And we didn't. And the misery of that day is still with me. I won't love somebody like that again, Kara. I won't risk it."

"I'm so sorry," she said as one stray tear escaped the corner of her eye and trickled down her cheek. "For Mac. For all of you." She inhaled sharply and added, "And I'm sorry for us."

Then she turned, walked back to the bed and closed her suitcase. She zipped it shut, the sound overly loud in the strained silence. Picking it up, she slung her purse over her shoulder and turned for one last look at Cooper.

"I'm going to your grandfather's. Maggie said I could stay in the guesthouse until my flight tomorrow night."

"You don't have to leave."

"Yes," she said, "I really do."

She walked to the open doorway and paused on the threshold to look back at him again. His gaze was locked on her and she wished desperately she could know what he was thinking, feeling. But Cooper had become too adept at hiding those feelings from everyone—including himself—to give anything away now.

"Be happy, Cooper," she said, then turned and walked away.

Eleven

Cooper was still standing where she'd left him, dumbfounded by the fact that Kara had actually gone, when he heard the front door open, then swing shut behind her. Silence pounded through the old house like hammer blows. He couldn't believe it. Kara. Gone.

Her image still fresh in his mind, he saw the hurt in her eyes and closed his own in a futile attempt to make that vision disappear. Instead, it became more clear.

"Damn it," he whispered into the empty room, feeling more alone than he ever had before. "I'd love you if I could, Kara. But it's too late for us."

Instantly, icy cold dropped onto the room as if an invisible blizzard was blowing through. Wind whistled around him, punching at him, driving him toward the doorway. His hair lifted in the swirling, chilly blast and he grabbed the doorjamb and hung on.

Throat tight, heart pounding, he looked around the bedroom in disbelief. A roar rose up with the wind and became a wild, frantic moan of pain. Framed pictures lifted off the walls and sailed in a wide, frigid circle. The overhead light flickered on and off in a frenzied flash like a strobe light in a nightclub. The mirror over the dresser shattered and reflective shards snapped into the room, landing on the floor in a tumble of jagged pieces.

Cooper let go of the doorjamb and braced his feet, leaning into the overpowering wind, determined to stand his own against the fury of the ghost. He stared at the mess and shouted to be heard above the wind, his breath misting in front of his face. "Knock it off! I don't owe you anything, you know!"

The wild keening became louder still and raised goose bumps on his flesh. His stomach dropped and he swallowed back a knot of pure adrenaline pumping through him. The painful, throbbing moan seemed to slice into his soul with an agony that was too deep for description.

And still the wind howled, pictures whirled in ever tightening circles and frost formed on the inside of the windows.

"She's gone and I can't stop her!"

More wailing, higher pitched, frantic.

The walls trembled and the wind screamed.

"I don't take orders from ghosts," he shouted, still trying to make himself heard. But even as those words sounded out in the room, a part of his brain argued with him.

Didn't he take orders from ghosts?

Wasn't everything he did because of Mac's ghost? Or at least the memory of him and what had happened so long ago?

Confusion rattled him and he staggered against the force of the cold battering at him. Was he really so different from the ghost trapped in this house?

Like him, hadn't she given up everything because of her own pain? Hadn't she spent the rest of her life, locked away in grief? Even in death, she stayed determined to shut out even the spirit of the man who was still trying to reach her.

She was so caught up in her own misery, she wasn't able to see a way out. Not then. Not now.

And suddenly, his own possible future stretched out in front of him and that, more than the ghostly cold, chilled Cooper to the bone.

"No," he muttered, shoving both hands through his hair and feeling the ice on his own fingertips. He wasn't like this trapped ghost. His situation was different.

But was it?

He'd cut himself off from love to protect himself from more pain. Kara had tried to get in, past the walls he'd put up around his heart and he'd shut her out. Hadn't this ghost done the same damn thing?

Wasn't she *still* doing it?

The wind abruptly died and the whirling pictures dropped to the floor with a clatter. The cold eased back and rivulets of water traced through the suddenly melting frost on the glass, as if the house were crying.

As the temperature in the room climbed back to normal Cooper stood stunned, like a survivor of a battle, and tried to make sense of his own thoughts.

Before it really was too late.

When a vehicle pulled into Jeremiah's yard an hour after she'd gone to bed, Kara sensed that it was Cooper. She lay awake, staring at the ceiling. She refused to get up and go to the window. Refused to look at him one more time, knowing that if she did, her resolve to leave would only weaken.

And she couldn't allow that.

Couldn't spend the rest of her life, waiting for Cooper to wake up and see that he had a right to live. To love.

So she burrowed under the quilt and willed herself into a restless sleep.

Cooper pounded on the back door of his grandfather's house. He glanced across the yard to the darkened guesthouse and fought the urge to go over there. To pound on the door and demand that Kara let him in.

Desperation ticked inside him like an over-wound clock. Turning back to the door in front of him, he pounded on it again, hard wood stinging his knuckles. He felt a tightly coiled spring inside him and wondered what would happen when it finally snapped.

When the door flew open, he staggered back a step and damn near fell off the back porch.

"Are you *nuts?*" Sam demanded, glaring at Cooper in the harsh glow of the porch light. "What the hell are you doing waking me up?"

"I need to talk to you." Cooper ignored his cousin's temper and pushed past Sam into the lamp lit kitchen. His sneakers squeaked on the linoleum as he paced a frantic route back and forth between the sink and the refrigerator. Stabbing his fingers through his hair repeatedly, he tried to shake loose the tumbling thoughts rolling through his brain, but he just couldn't make sense of them.

Which was why he'd come to Sam.

Sam had been there that day.

Sam knew what Cooper was living with because he had to live with it, too. But somehow, Sam had made it past the ugliness of that one day fifteen years ago. He'd made peace with Mac and Cooper desperately needed to know how he'd done it.

The door closed and Cooper looked at his cousin. Wearing only a pair of drawstring pajama bottoms,

Sam leaned back against the door, folded his arms across his bare chest and demanded, "What the hell is wrong with you, Cooper?"

"Nothing," he muttered, then corrected himself. "Everything."

"I'm gonna need more," Sam demanded, then headed to the fridge. Pulling out a jug of orange juice, he walked to a cupboard, took out two glasses and poured each of them a drink. Taking a sip, he said, "And keep it down, will you? Maggie spent most of the night heaving her guts up and she needs the rest."

"Sorry," Cooper said automatically, holding the small juice glass cupped in both palms. "But I had to see you."

"Okay," Sam said, picking up on the desperation wafting off Cooper in thick waves. He sat down at the table, pointed to a chair and said, "So here I am. Talk."

Cooper ignored the chair. He couldn't have sat still at the moment if his life had depended on it. Instead, he took a gulp of the OJ and said, "How'd you do it?"

"Do what?"

"Get past what happened to Mac." Cooper's gaze fixed on Sam in a steady stare. "I know you, Sam. You've spent the last fifteen years just like I have— just like Jake has. Avoiding family. Avoiding each other. All because of what happened that day."

Sam's gaze dropped to the glass of juice. "Yeah. I did."

"So what changed?"

He lifted his gaze again and shrugged. "I found Maggie."

"And just like that you could open up? You could change who you were?"

"Hell, no," Sam said, slumping back against the chair. "I didn't want to change. Didn't want to love her. Didn't want to stay here," he said, waving one hand to encompass the house, the ranch and all of Coleville. "But damn it, Cooper, I was tired of running from Mac."

"Is that what we're doing?" he asked thoughtfully. "Or are we running from what we didn't do that day?"

"A little of both, I think," Sam said. "Sit down, Cooper."

Slowly, Cooper sank onto the chair but kept his gaze fixed on his cousin. Quietly, he said, "Kara's leaving."

"I know."

"Of course you know," Cooper said with a strained chuckle. "She's *here.*"

"And are you letting her go?"

"I can't stop her." It tore at him. Everything in him wanted to leave this house, march across the yard and pound on the door of the guesthouse until she let him in. He wanted to bury himself inside her and let her warmth wrap around him.

But how could he do that?

"You're an idiot."

Cooper's gaze snapped back to Sam's. "Thanks. I feel better."

Leaning forward, bracing both arms on the tabletop, Sam shook his head and said, "You shouldn't feel better. Kara's leaving and you're not doing anything to prevent it. You should feel horrible."

"I do," Cooper admitted. "But damn it, how can I love her? How the hell can I do that after Mac?"

"What's Mac got to do with it?"

"You're a great one to say that."

"Right. Okay. I get it. But I got past that," Sam said. "I almost lost Maggie. Almost lost the child we made together." He shook his head slowly, in disbelief, as if even *he* could hardly understand the man who'd made so many bad choices. "Do you really think Mac would have wanted that? Do you believe Mac wants us all to suffer for the rest of our lives?"

"No, I don't," Cooper said grudgingly. God, he could still see Mac so clearly in his mind. Forever sixteen years old, his eyes shining with mischief, his wild laugh punching the air as he challenged his cousins to one daredevil stunt after another.

Mac had loved life so much. Had squeezed every drop of fun out of every damn day he'd had. He'd hate knowing his cousins had pretty much resigned from life because of him.

"But how do you get past the fear?" Cooper asked quietly, studying the surface of the orange juice as if it had the secrets of the world etched on top. "How do you let yourself love somebody that freely again without being terrified of losing it?"

"You don't," Sam said, just as quietly. "The fear's always there. I can't even imagine losing Maggie. The thought of it terrifies me."

"Comforting."

"But the love's always there, too," Sam told him. "And without that, all you've got is the fear. That's an empty way to live, Cooper."

"Yeah."

"So, if you came here looking for advice…here it is." Sam stood up and looked down at him. "Make peace with Mac. Lay the past to rest so you can have a future."

"I don't know that I can."

"If you can't…" Sam said, "If you're willing to let Kara go out of your life because you're too scared to let her in—"

"Yeah?"

"—Then you don't deserve her anyway." He picked up his orange juice, drained it, then set the glass on the kitchen counter. "Turn off the light and lock the door when you go."

Cooper knew the way to the lake.

Could have found his way there blindfolded.

Time ticked past though as it took him more than twice as long to walk the distance as it should have. Every step felt as though he were dragging his feet free of mud. His brain knew he had to go back to the lake—face what had happened so long ago.

But his heart ached at the thought of it.

Fifteen years had passed, but the land hadn't changed much. He slowly climbed the ridge in the pale wash of moonlight and in the distance, heard the high-pitched howl of a coyote serenade. A soft, cool wind with the taste of the ocean on it, swept across the open fields and tugged at Cooper's hair. He turned his face into it and paused long enough to settle the frantic race of his heartbeat.

He'd never intended to come back here. To this place. Never thought he'd be able to.

And as he made it to the top of the ridge and looked out over the dark water, dappled in moonlight, he felt the years pass away. Once again, he was sixteen, standing with his cousins at the top of the world.

He felt the sun, hot on his bare shoulders. Heard Jake cussing a blue streak because Mac had out-jumped him. Listened to Sam chuckle as he carefully studied the stopwatch, timing Mac's underwater stretch. And heard himself saying *Give him another few seconds, Sam. He really wants to beat Jake. And I want him to. Mac's okay. Stop being an old woman.*

Wincing now, Cooper stared out at the spot where Mac had landed that last time. And he kept staring, as if he could see through the water to where they'd eventually found Mac, stretched out on the bottom of the lake—already dead.

They'd tried CPR. They'd tried pushing the water from Mac's lungs.

But they were too late.

And they'd lost not only Mac that afternoon, but their own innocence and sense of invincibility.

"Mac?" Cooper's whisper came low and strained, as if that single word had been squeezed out of his throat grudgingly. "You still here?"

The wind pushed at him playfully and in his mind, he heard laughter. Mac's laughter. Cooper spun around, half expecting to see the tall, lanky kid striding up the ridge to join him.

And the disappointment at finding himself all alone was staggering.

Still, remembering the furious temper of the ghost he'd left behind at the Victorian, Cooper wondered if Mac's spirit was trapped at the lake. Was he here, even now, waiting for his cousins to come back and—*what?*

"What could you be waiting for? To hear us say we're sorry?" he asked the wind. "What good would that do?"

Toward the east, the sky was beginning to lighten into a soft violet, heralding the coming dawn. Hours must have passed since he'd left the ranch house. Amazing that he'd been walking for so long.

He lifted his gaze from the rippled surface of the lake to the star-studded sky overhead. "We *are* sorry, you know. For all the good it does. You died too young, Mac. And we miss you. All of us do."

Shaking his head, he admitted, "God, I've relived that day a thousand times. Over and over again in my mind, I've replayed what happened. And every time, I save you." His voice broke and his gaze dropped, back to the lake, where his young life had shattered so completely.

"I want you to know that, Mac. Every time I remember that day, we save you." He choked out a laugh and rubbed his hand across his face. "Of course, we didn't when it really counted…God, I wish I could change it. Wish I could bring you back. Or hell, even talk to you. I've missed you so damn much."

A freshening wind slapped at him again, throwing his hair across his eyes and he found himself smiling in spite of the knife-like pain twisting inside him. Was the wind Mac's way of telling him to stop beating himself up over the past?

Or was that just wishful thinking?

Hell, up to a few weeks ago, Cooper had never really believed in ghosts. Now, he was convinced that something of who you were survived death. It wasn't a complete end. Maybe death really was just a bend in the road, beyond which we can't see. Maybe there's more out there than any of us have ever imagined.

God, he hoped so.

Hoped Mac was having a great time wherever he was. But could he move on, knowing that those he'd left behind were all still trapped in reruns of that summer day?

Cooper had never known pain like he'd experienced that day fifteen years before. Because he'd deliberately avoided it. By never allowing himself to love that freely, deeply, he'd kept himself free from pain—but he'd also hidden away from real joy. He'd lived a half life—safe but alone. Hell, Mac had lived more in sixteen years than Cooper had in thirty-one.

He'd locked himself away from life in some self-appointed penance for something he couldn't have changed. He'd felt guilty being alive when Mac was dead. And maybe, he thought, if something of Mac lingered in this place, maybe it was because none of his cousins had been able to let him go.

He'd hate to think that.

The three of them—Cooper, Sam and Jake—had all grieved in their own way, but they'd all shared at least one trait. They'd stayed away. From here.

From memories of Mac.

Yet, there'd been so much more to Mac than that one last day. And instead of focusing on those memories, they'd all chosen to relive the tragedy over and over again.

What a waste.

What a pitiful way to remember a boy they'd all loved.

Suddenly exhausted as emotions churned inside, Cooper dropped onto the grassy ground, drew his knees up and wrapped his arms around them. In the moonlight and the still chill of the night, Cooper felt the ice around his heart shatter and fall away. The cold he'd lived with for so long began to melt and he drew his first easy breath in fifteen long years.

Stretching out on the dewy grass, Cooper closed his eyes and felt the exhaustion of the complete release of tension seep through him like a rising tide. The aches and misery of years washed away, leaving him with only the memories of the good times they'd all had.

Of the summers that would live forever.

Of the boy who'd died too young, but had lived a lifetime in sixteen short years.

And in his mind, he saw Mac again. Young and laughing. Running up the ridge and leaping out into the lake—fearless, joyful.

Cooper smiled and whispered, "Thanks, Mac."

Twelve

Cooper woke with a jolt.

Sunlight streamed into his eyes and he squinted instantly in self-defense. A moment or two of complete confusion rattled through him. Where the hell was he and how did he—

The lake. He sat straight up and stared down from the ridge at the dark blue water below. Sunlight skittered off the surface, twinkling like downed stars.

He rubbed his eyes and stood up, stretching aching muscles. Not the most comfortable place to spend the night, he thought, but at the same time, it had been the best sleep he'd had in fifteen years. He'd finally come to terms with Mac.

Sorrow balled in the pit of his stomach, but this was a sweet sadness for something long missed. Not the lurch of guilt and pain that had so long been a part of his life.

"Kara was right," he said aloud, then shot a quick look at his watch. *Kara.*

She was leaving and he had to stop her. Had to try to make her see that he wasn't a complete loss. That he'd finally found a way to look ahead. To look into his own future and when he did, all he saw was her.

Then, as if Mac were standing right there beside him, he heard his cousin's voice say, *What're you waiting for? Go get her.*

Grinning, Cooper turned around and started running toward the ranch—toward Kara.

"Thanks for the ride," Kara said, reaching into the backseat to pull out her suitcase.

"Not a problem," Maggie told her and closed the door for her. "But are you sure about this? You've got a long day of just sitting at the airport waiting for your plane."

Kara inhaled sharply, deeply and glanced around at the people jostling for space at curb side check-in. Then she shifted her gaze back to Maggie. The woman stared at her with sympathy in her eyes, and though Kara appreciated the thought, she really didn't want to acknowledge it. And, if she'd spent the day at the ranch, she'd have been faced with that sympathy all day. Not only from Maggie, but from Sam and Jeremiah and even Jake.

And, there was always the chance that Cooper might drop by the ranch house. No. It was better this way. She'd rather spend the day at the airport than risk running into Cooper one more time.

"Don't worry about me," she chirped, putting a little too much cheer into her voice, "I've got a good book and a pile of magazines to read."

Maggie nodded as if she understood every thought that was racing through Kara's mind. "Okay. But if it's okay with you, when I get back to the ranch, I think I'll give Cooper a good hard kick."

Unexpectedly, a sheen of tears bristled at the backs of her eyes and Kara smiled tightly. "Thanks," she said and instinctively leaned in for a hug. Then before she could change her mind, she grabbed hold of the suitcase handle and headed for the terminal.

"Kara!" Cooper pounded on the door of the guesthouse, then moved to the front window. Stepping through the jungle of geraniums planted before it, he cupped his hands on the window glass and peered into the dark house. "Kara, damn it, open the door! I need to talk to you!"

Nothing.

"What the hell are you up to?" Sam called out from across the yard.

Cooper spun around. "I'm looking for Kara. Where is she?"

Sam leaned one shoulder against a porch post and lifted a cup of coffee for a sip. "She came here to get away from you, Cooper."

Pushing through the geraniums that fought him every inch of the way, Cooper stomped across the grassy dirt and stood at the bottom of the steps, glaring at his cousin. "Don't get in the middle of this, Sam."

"Get in?" Sam countered with a sneer, "You're the one who *dragged* me in, remember? Weren't you just here last night complaining to me?"

"Yeah," he admitted. "I was." Scraping one hand along the side of his head, he pushed his hair back then let his hand drop in disgust. "But things're different now. I—" He shut up suddenly and demanded, "Where is she?"

"She's gone."

"Gone?" Panic bubbled up in his throat but Cooper swallowed it. "What do you mean, *gone?*"

"What's all the shouting about?" Jeremiah demanded, stepping out onto the porch beside Sam. "Oh, Cooper. It's you."

"Yeah, it's me."

Sheba hurtled out the back door, squeezing through the legs of the two men to throw herself joyfully at Cooper. Bounding at his legs, she yapped and barked and ran in dizzying circles around him in a bid for attention. Cooper was too focused to notice.

"Man, can't a guy even get any sleep in the country?" Jake's grumble rolled over the puppy's gleeful barking in a growl of complaint. "I've slept in train stations quieter than this place."

"Great." Cooper threw his hands high, then let them fall again. "Everybody here now?" Narrowing a look at Sam, he demanded, "Where's Kara?"

"Why should I tell you?"

Jake grabbed Sam's coffee and took a long gulp.

"Hey, get your own."

Jake ignored him, only mumbling, "Tell him where she is, already, huh? And somebody shut that dog up."

"Still a prizewinner in the morning, aren't you?" Jeremiah snapped, then said, "Sheba! Cut it out."

The puppy immediately quieted and plopped her butt onto the ground beside Cooper, all the while managing to still wag her tail and squirm in place.

"Damn it Sam, tell me," Cooper said, ignoring the others. "Please."

Sam studied him for a long minute before making up his mind. Finally though, he nodded, took his cup back from Jake and looked at Cooper. "Maggie took her to the airport. She went early I think, to avoid seeing you again."

Cooper winced as the truth of that statement hit him like a slap. God, he'd been an idiot. The question was, was it too late to make up for it?

"Thanks," he said and headed for Jeremiah's beat-up ranch truck. "I'll bring the truck back later."

"Boy," Jeremiah shouted, taking the first couple of steps. "Wait up a minute there. I've got something I've got to say to the three of you and—"

Cooper never even looked back. "It'll have to wait, Jeremiah." He opened the truck door, climbed inside and fired up the engine. Slamming the door shut again, he threw the car into Drive, punched the gas pedal and muttered, "I've got something way more important to say. I only hope she'll listen."

"Hey!" A security guard shouted as Cooper parked the truck in front of the terminal and bailed out. "You can't leave that thing there!"

He didn't have time to move it. Didn't care enough to worry about it. His brain was focused on one thing. Kara. She was all that mattered now.

She was *all*.

"Have it towed," he shouted back and hit the automatic double doors in such a hurry they didn't have time to swing open for him. He'd worry about the truck later. Pay the fines, whatever.

Right now, he had to find her.

His gaze swept the crowd. People. Too many people. The noise level was immense. Kids cried, parents soothed, teenagers up against a wall, kissing goodbye as if facing Armageddon. Huge suitcases rolled across the gleaming linoleum, their steel wheels growling a warning at anyone in their way. A disembodied voice shimmied through the speaker system, but the words were garbled, as if the speaker was talking around a mouthful of marbles.

Cooper's gaze swung back and forth, searching every face. Stalking through the crowd, pushing through the congested terminal, he checked the television screens for arrival and departure times and located the gate that Kara's plane would be using.

He sprinted down the long, narrow passage, slipping in and out of the crowd, mumbling apologies, but never stopping. Never slowing. His heart raced and his brain moved even faster. One speech after another rose up in his mind, was considered, then rejected. He had to make her see. Understand.

Had to make her *believe*.

But how?

Just outside security, his gaze shifted quickly over the people standing in line until he found the one face he'd been searching for. Kara. She stood alone, staring into space.

His heart twisted in his chest and he swallowed hard. This was it. And if he blew it, he'd never forgive himself.

Hurrying to her, he stopped right in front of her and waited as she slowly lifted her gaze to his. He saw surprise and pleasure light up her eyes before those emotions were extinguished and buried under a sheen of regret.

He felt the solid punch of her pain as if it were a blow to his midsection, but he couldn't let it stop him. "I've been looking for you," he said inanely.

"I left the ranch early so I wouldn't have to see you again," she admitted.

"Yeah, I figured that out. And I don't blame you," he said. Reaching for her hands, he held them in both of his and tightened his grip when she would have pulled free. "Don't. Kara, please. You've gotta listen to me."

Hope lit up her eyes briefly, then was gone again in a wink. But the fact that it had been there at all, gave Cooper reason for a little hope himself.

"I really think we've said everything, Cooper."

"Not by a long shot," he argued, then fixed a steely stare on a businessman type who wandered up to take his place in line behind her. The man got the message and scuttled off quickly.

"Fine," she said. "Say what you came to say and then go, okay?"

"I'm an idiot."

Both of her eyebrows lifted. "Interesting start."

He gave her a half smile and squeezed her hands briefly. "There's more."

"I'm listening," she said and he could see her take a deep breath and hold it.

Shaking his head, Cooper searched for the right words but couldn't find them. "Damn it, I'm a writer.

I should be good at this. But now, when I need them the most, the words aren't there."

Hope was back in her eyes and just a hint of a smile was on her mouth. "Give it your best shot."

"Okay." Nodding, he said, "I'll say the most important part first and work back around to it again later."

She nodded, waiting.

"I love you."

She sucked in a gulp of air and tears began to glitter in her eyes. Panic jolted inside him.

"I don't want you to cry," he said desperately. "I wanted to make you happy. Make *us* happy."

"Then keep talking," she urged.

"You were right," he said, figuring every woman loved to hear that—especially when it was true. "I should have told you about Mac. Hell, I should have found a way to deal with that pain a long time ago. But I didn't. Because it was easier to hide from it. To hide from everything. Everyone."

She squeezed his hands. In support? Sympathy? He didn't know, so he kept talking.

"I hid from life for so long, Kara," he said, "I'd forgotten what real joy was. What life could be like. But the last week or so with you reminded me. I know we've been together for a long time, but here, it was different. In Coleville, we were really *together,* together. You know?"

"Yeah, I know what you mean."

"Good. Good." He nodded and fought for breath.

That voice over the loudspeaker came again and all over the airport, heads cocked to listen, to try to understand the garbled words. The security line moved forward.

Cooper and Kara ignored it.

"I went to the lake last night."

"You did?" Understanding lit up her eyes and highlighted the banked tears about to fall.

Cooper talked faster, hoping to forestall them.

"I did. I talked to Mac. Discovered something else you were right about. It wasn't our fault. And Mac doesn't blame us."

"Oh, Cooper…"

"I think he wants us to be happy," he was saying, feeling the truth of his words as they poured from him in a rush. "I think he expects us to live the kind of life he would have if he'd been given the chance. And Kara, I want that, too."

"I'm glad."

"Good," he said smiling, "because you're pretty much integral to my plan."

"I am?" Her fingers curled around his and he lifted their joined hands to kiss her knuckles.

"Oh, you really are. I love you, Kara. See? Told you I'd get back around to the most important part of this."

"I'm liking it so far."

He swallowed a knot of emotion so huge it threatened to choke him, but still he found a way to say,

"I never thought I could love this much. But I do. You're everything to me, Kara. And I want the chance to prove it to you."

"Cooper…"

He spoke fast, half afraid she'd shut him down before he could finish. "No, listen. I won't let you go without a fight, Kara. If you get on a plane, I'll follow you. If you move, I'll go wherever you do. I will spend the rest of my life proving to you just how much I love you. If you'll just give me that chance."

Kara's heart swelled in her chest so that she could hardly draw breath. This was everything and more than she'd ever hoped for. And oh, she wanted to believe. She looked into Cooper's eyes and read the very emotions she'd so hoped to see. But she had to have more.

She wasn't prepared to settle for less than everything.

"I love you, too, Cooper," she said.

"Thank God," he murmured, shoulders slumping in relief.

"But…"

"There's a but?"

She smiled at him. "I won't settle for being your assistant or live-in lover. I want it all, Cooper. I want to be married. I want kids. A family."

He gave her a grin that nearly knocked her off her feet. "Of course we'll get married. And we'll have dozens of kids!"

"Dozens?"

"That part's negotiable," he acknowledged, then added, "and you won't be my assistant anymore. We'll hire someone else."

Kara shook her head and leaned in for a long, lingering kiss. "Nobody butters your toast but me, Cooper."

He sighed and drew her into the circle of his arms. "Now that sounds like a plan." After a quick hug, though, he pulled back and said, "Come on. I'm taking you back to the house. We've got a lot of making up to do."

"Now *that's* a plan," she said, throwing his own words back at him.

They had to take a cab, since Jeremiah's truck had indeed been towed. But Cooper promised to ransom it... *later*.

He carried her up the short flight of steps to the front door, but before he could open it, the heavy wood door swung open in invitation. Tightening his grip on Kara, Cooper cautiously stepped into the foyer and stopped dead.

Warmth spilled through the old house and sunlight seemed to spear in directly through the walls, making the whole place brilliant with a hazy, golden glow as unearthly as it was beautiful.

"What?" Cooper whispered.

"Shh..." Kara urged, smiling. "Listen."

Cooper held his breath and waited. Then he heard the soft, musical sound that Kara had.

A young couple, laughing with unrestrained joy. Together at last.

Epilogue

The truck had been bailed out of the storage yard, Kara's already checked suitcase would be returned as soon as it reached New York and she and Cooper had already made quite an effort at starting their first child.

After dinner at Jeremiah's, the family sat around the kitchen table and waited for the older man to make the announcement he'd called them all together for.

At last, he stood up, and looked from one grandson to the other. "I can't tell you boys what it means to this old man to have you all home again." Then he smiled at Kara and Maggie in turn. "And to have you two in my family, makes me gladder than you'll ever know."

Kara reached for Cooper's hand and her heart skipped when he folded his fingers around it.

"But beyond missing you all," Jeremiah said, "there was another reason for getting you back here this summer."

"You're not going to try the 'I'm dying' thing again, are you?" Jake asked.

"Nope." Jeremiah had the grace to flush and in the overhead kitchen light, his eyes sparkled with something that looked a lot like expectation. "This is the God's truth. And I decided to wait until all three of you were here together to tell you."

"C'mon, Jeremiah," Sam urged, dropping one arm around Maggie's shoulders. "Spill it before you bust."

"Right then. Donna Barrett's back in town."

"I know," Cooper said. "I saw her at the drugstore. Hell, I'm the one who told you guys. So if that's your news, Jeremiah, it's a little late."

The old man scowled at him. "There's more. She didn't come back to town alone. She's got Mac's son with her."

* * * * *

Maureen Child's SUMMER OF SECRETS
comes to an end with
SATISFYING LONERGAN'S HONOR,
available in June from Silhouette Desire.

HOTEL MARCHAND

Four sisters.
A family legacy.
And someone is out to destroy it.

A captivating new limited continuity, launching June 2006

The most beautiful hotel in New Orleans,
and someone is out to destroy it. But mystery,
danger and some surprising family revelations
and discoveries won't stop the Marchand sisters
from protecting their birthright…
and finding love along the way.

SPECIAL PRICE!

This riveting new saga begins with

In the Dark

by national bestselling author

JUDITH ARNOLD

The party at Hotel Marchand is in full swing when the lights suddenly go out. What does head of security Mac Jensen do first? He's torn between two jobs—protecting the guests at the hotel and keeping the woman he loves safe.

A woman to protect. A hotel to secure. And no idea who's determined to harm them.

On Sale June 2006

Page-turning drama...

Exotic, glamorous locations...

Intense emotion and passionate seduction...

Sheikhs, princes and billionaire tycoons...

This summer, may we suggest:

THE SHEIKH'S DISOBEDIENT BRIDE
by Jane Porter
On sale June.

AT THE GREEK TYCOON'S BIDDING
by Cathy Williams
On sale July.

THE ITALIAN MILLIONAIRE'S VIRGIN WIFE
On sale August.

With new titles to choose from every month,
discover a world of romance in our books written
by internationally bestselling authors.

HARLEQUIN® *Presents*

It's the ultimate in quality romance!

Available wherever Harlequin books are sold.

www.eHarlequin.com

HPGEN06

Paying the Playboy's Price

(Silhouette Desire #1732)

by

EMILIE ROSE

Juliana Alden is determined to have her last—
her only—fling before settling down. And she's
found the perfect candidate: bachelor Rex Tanner.
He's pure playboy charm…but can she afford
his price?

Trust Fund Affairs: They've just spent a fortune—
the bachelors had better be worth it.

Don't miss the other titles in this series:

EXPOSING THE EXECUTIVE'S SECRETS (July)
BENDING TO THE BACHELOR'S WILL (August)

On sale this June from Silhouette Desire.

*Available wherever books are sold, including most
bookstores, supermarkets, discount stores and drugstores.*

COMING NEXT MONTH

#1729 HEIRESS BEWARE—Charlene Sands
The Elliotts
She was about to expose her family's darkest secrets, but then she lost her memory and found herself in a stranger's arms.

**#1730 SATISFYING LONERGAN'S HONOR—
Maureen Child**
Summer of Secrets
Their passion had been denied for far too many years. But will secrets of a long-ago summer come between them once more?

**#1731 THE SOON-TO-BE-DISINHERITED WIFE—
Jennifer Greene**
Secret Lives of Society Wives
He didn't know if their romantic entanglement was real, or a ruse in order to secure her multimillion-dollar inheritance.

#1732 PAYING THE PLAYBOY'S PRICE—Emilie Rose
Trust Fund Affairs
Desperate to break free of her good-girl image, this society sweetheart bought herself a bachelor at an auction. But what would her stunt really cost her?

#1733 FORCED TO THE ALTAR—Susan Crosby
Rich and Reclusive
Her only refuge was his dark and secretive home. His only salvation was her acceptance of his proposal.

#1734 A CONVENIENT PROPOSITION—Cindy Gerard
Pregnant and alone, she entered into a marriage of convenience... never imagining her attraction to her new husband would prove so *in*convenient.

SDCNM0506